BENEATH THE SURFACE OF LIGHT

Acknowledgments

I would first and foremost like to thank my mother who motivated me to keep writing, believed in my story and in me. Thank you for always standing by my side and for all your sacrifices. I hope I make you proud.

Thank you to my sister for showing me that being the weird one in the crowd is more than okay and to my brothers who are always there with a word of wisdom when I get stuck. I am eternally grateful for my badass goddess friends, Sarah, Lyla, Mish, Eva, Gail and Daria. I love you all to bits. Thank you for inspiriting me to live an authentic life and for showing me that the answer is always love.

My dear friend Heather, for your kindness and the community you created and let me be a part of. Thank you for your countless proofreads. Your patience and dedication have been greatly appreciated. I want to thank Christine and our shared vision. Your front cover design was spot on the first time.

A big thank you to Ms.Connolly. Your way of exploring 'The Great Gatsby' with us has inspired my love for the English language. I think of you often. Thank you to my teachers in Ecuador and India. You helped shine a light on my path to finding my purpose and the path home back to myself. There is a special place in my heart for you Rosa, and Prashant.

Thank you to my contributors who helped me finance my first editor. Without you, the story would have ended at fifty thousand words. Christine, Lisa, Jose, Bianca, Maria, Ruby, Basia, Lottie, Karolis, Michaela, Pedro, Adriana, Ian, Kasia, Helen, Fiona, Amaryllis, Kris, Sonia, Shane, Katie, Michelle, and special thanks to Ramil. Thank you, Savannah. Your vision for the book made it all possible. Thank you, Brian. Your humour is one of a kind. Thank you, Melissa. Your enthusiasm and encouragement were priceless.

I am grateful for the love I have received and the people that had helped me embrace the feeling of belonging to something greater than myself. My yogis, my lightworkers, my dear friends, Angela. Thank you to all that have guided me and held me through the dark times. I wouldn't be here if it wasn't for you. And thank you to one who has pushed me deeper on my own self-love journey. You helped me grow in ways I never could on my own.

Thank you, universe. Thank you, divine timing.

CHAPTER 1

THE REAL AND THE IMAGINED

Spring. It was Whalina's favourite season. After a long and grey winter, the gentle sunrays and crispy air made her feel alive once again. Together with the yellow daffodils, she felt herself bloom. The emergence of life in nature stimulated her mind. Rabbits came out their holes, and birds were confident to bring young ones into the world, transforming dead twigs and branches into their new homes.

Whalina heard the enchanting birdsong first that morning. Under the warm cotton sheets, she envisioned the bird concert outside her window, the robins and the blue jays sitting next to one another, the black and white magpies singing their hearts out, and an owl taking the role of principal conductor to ensure no one flew out of tune. Even the crows joined as they played the violins, and the eagles proudly watched the spectacle. Such a scene was only possible in the early hours of the morning, reserved for those who rose with the sun.

Whalina opened her eyes to check the bedside, avocado-shaped alarm clock—half past six. She faced Neal, who was a deep sleeper and always slept longer than her. She watched him for a moment, wondering what he was dreaming of, before plucking a white feather from the dreamcatcher that hung on the bedframe above. Trying to contain her laughter, Whalina slowly manoeuvred the soft feather around his nose, watching it twitch and his eyes flicker. Oblivious to her heart beating faster, she became deeply engrossed in the moment. The excitement built inside her, and she was ready to fall into his arms the second he opened his eyes. Yet, as with most things in life, we were never quite as ready as we imagined.

While she was lost in the moment, Neal startled Whalina as he roared like a bear, wrapping his arms around her.

Whalina finally released the laughter that had been building inside her, filling the room with childlike innocence.

"You have no idea how much I wanted to laugh," she said, giggling.

"I heard you move for at least ten minutes, Ali. I was waiting to see how long before you lost your patience," he said with his deep morning voice.

"Come on! Get up and let's hit the road before the whole of London wakes up," she said, jumping out of bed.

*****

Twenty minutes later, they were both ready and on the road, driving with the windows down. Whalina's dark brown hair blew in all directions, screaming for freedom. The warm air carried a sense of abundance, intoxicating the passengers who were singing carelessly to Queen. Their youthful energy bounced off one another in an epic duo of the modern Bonnie and Clyde or Sid and Nancy, minus the drugs and the murderers. Neal and Whalina were what the millennials would call 'couple goals.' They shared a genuine love, with qualities of patience and acceptance—something the older generations considered the norm, rare in the era of mobile phones and disconnection. Their love affair could be considered, in many ways, as cliché or young, yet, from the beginning, it had carried a particular essence of knowing and belonging. It was a love made to last, and they knew it.

Neal was driving his 1968 Ford Mustang to the far west of the island for what was forecasted as a relaxing weekend getaway. They would often venture outside the loud city scene to be with nature, trees, and water.

After a five-hour car journey, Whalina could hardly sit still as the two-storey, detached granite house came to view. It was in a secluded part of Cornwall, allowing for solitude and privacy. Greenery, ranging from white clovers to bluebells, surrounded the cottage, offering glimpses of the Cornish countryside visible from the back of the house through the gaps that the sessile oaks allowed between them. Although beautiful, Whalina preferred the breath-taking views seen from the stone porch stairs. Neal had a way of always bringing Whalina back to Earth; he inspired a sense of calm and peace within. He felt home to her, more than she ever felt home inside her own skin.

Whalina found her way back to her body and swam to shore without taking her focus off Neal. He finally looked back, and his smile released the dense steam from her chest. All she needed was for him to see her. As she emerged from the sea, the cool air hit her wet skin, and she wrapped herself in a beach towel while lazily running in the sand to the small, garden glass table where Neal was waiting with coffee.

"Good morning, sunshine," he said as Whalina sat in his lap. His large arms wrapped tightly around her, and he didn't seem to mind that she was dripping wet.

"It happened again," she whispered, as though saying it quietly made it somewhat less real.

"A panic attack?" Whalina could hear him trying to sound empathetic.

"It's not a panic attack. It feels too real," she answered, apprehensively unsure whether it was possible for him to understand.

"Maybe reconsider telling Pedro about this. He's a trained professional, sweethea—"

"No, I don't want my shrink thinking I'm crazy. I just need to understand what is happening to me." Whalina allowed herself to surrender deeper into Neal's embrace.

"I don't want to think about it today, okay?" she aimed to ask but sounded more like a non-negotiable demand.

"I know what will get your mind off things. Go on and get dressed. I'll meet you outside in ten." He clapped his hands and ushered Whalina inside the house.

A few minutes later, she came out of the house, wearing a knee-length lemon-coloured dress she had bought in one of the local charity shops a few years back. It was one of her favourites because it was comfortable and loose on the body.

"So, where are we going?" She took hold of Neal's hand as they walked barefoot alongside the coastline.

The sand was warm, and at last, the wind had settled.

"Waves Water Sports, Al," he said, smiling.

Whalina loved when he called her 'Al.' It was short for Alina, and nobody called her that apart from him. Her name was an unusual one, and only strangers called her Whalina. On the first day they met, he had told her she was extraordinary, out of this world, and even joked she was some sort of artificial intelligence being from a different planet. From Ai became Al, and each time he called her Al, she felt a tiny light switch go off in her chest. He made her feel special.

Waves Water Sports was a family-owned business they would visit on their every trip to Cornwall. As they approached the end of the pier, the music from the boat lowered, and Mark greeted them with a big grin. Mark was the youngest crewmember, a dedicated boat driver and water sports teacher. He first taught Whalina when they had visited Cornwall three years ago for their one-year anniversary.

Whalina sat at the back of the boat, enjoying the cool wind blowing through her wavy beach hair. The sun was beaming at solar noon in its highest position in the clear, blue sky, and as expected, the water was calm.

Once they built enough distance from the coast, Mark slowed down and said, "My bets are on Whalina going in first."

Whalina confirmed, nodding with excitement, and quickly took off her dress, revealing the stripy, white and navy-blue bathing suit she had put on before. Without hesitation, she jumped into the turquoise water.

Mark passed her the wakeboard and rope.

"Ready?"

"Ready!"

Mark switched the engine back on and slowly built speed. Without an ounce of hesitation, Whalina stood on the board, and a few moments later, she let go of the rope and rode the wave. Once Neal took a couple of pictures, he sat closer to Mark, and whilst they were talking, Whalina tested the water. She glided with ease, playing with the waves, dancing a water dance of going in and out of the wake, and bending her knees to touch the small waves that the boat was creating.

She thought if a species of human fish existed, this would be it. She imagined the board was an extension of her tail, and despite the boat going at no more than ten or eleven knots, in her head, she was an invincible wave rider. Engrossed in the ride, she knew there was nowhere she'd rather be.

CHAPTER 2

THE FIRST JOURNEY

One belief behind reincarnation is that before a child is born, the soul that is descending into the body will choose what they would like to learn and experience in their upcoming lifetime—what wounds they need to heal and what experiences they must have to advance their soul. During pre-incarnation, a soul agreement will take place, where life scenarios are conceived before birth. Souls choose relationships and family ties based on lessons they wish to learn in human form. One condition all souls must accept is that they must forfeit their memories and thus not remember why they had been born. Humans are spiritual beings having a human experience, and being human means having free will. Once one finds their true purpose, nothing and no one can stand in the way. Thus, the intent of living a human life would be defeated if we were all born already knowing what to do and how to do it.

Like all living beings on Earth, Whalina came here to remember her life's purpose and, most importantly, to fulfil that purpose. Such is life that some remember, whilst others die without ever knowing why they had lived. Their heart stops beating, the body dies, life as we know it is no more for the person whose body is decomposing. The deceased leaves family, friends, perhaps a lover, and all things mater-ial behind. They release their hopes and wishes into a graveyard of unfulfilled dreams, where they float aimlessly, knowing they will never come to fruition.

But the soul never dies. It cannot be destroyed, buried, or eaten by worms. It will go back home, a place of nourishment, rejuvenation, and unconditional love. It may rest there for years or return straight into a new body. The cycle of death and rebirth will continue until one has learnt their life lessons, and only then can one ascend into a realm beyond Earth. That's all that life is: a series of lessons for our souls to evolve. Life is eternal, but when the game is over and it's our time to go, nothing and no one can hold us back. Physical death is nothing but a form of pragmatism. One must simply let go of the attachments they have accumulated in their life so they can go on a new spiritual evolutionary adventure. Yet letting go of the one we love can be an impossible task.

*****

Whalina was desperate to see what the paramedics were doing to the love of her life. She struggled to understand the timeline of events, and time was ambiguous. The paramedics were leaning over Neal's body, and when Whalina tried to come closer, she lost control of her feet. It was as if she had been paralysed from the waist down. She couldn't reach out and hold his hand. People were walking, and their mouths were moving quickly, but there was no sound. Silence enclosed around her.

"Can someone please tell me what's going on?" she shouted in vain, for no one paid attention to the small voice. Whalina helplessly waved her hands to get one of the kind-faced paramedic's attention. Then her arms became numb. She stood frozen, unable to move or speak, confined to the cage of her consciousness, yet her mind could still experience pain. The bright ambulance lights shone in her eyes, forcing her to close them momentarily, and she entered a void. Darkness and stillness surrounded her, and when her eyes opened, it was again: the empty void of nonexistence.

At least now she could move her feet through what seemed to be a thick, heavy liquid. Whalina looked down to see what her feet were trudging through, but the darkness was impenetrable. She could not see her own body, and fear gripped her in a chokehold, for if no one could see her, not even herself, how could she be sure that she still existed? Whalina ran with what felt like sandbags on her legs through the deep vacuum of infinite blankness with no direction. Everywhere she looked was the same lifeless, empty nullity.

A small speck of light appeared on the distant horizon, like a falling star in the black sky, gifting Whalina with a pinch of hope. Running through the thick waters with all her strength felt like days, yet the light stayed small and untouchable. At last, she gave up, and the light went out. Darkness consumed whatever remained of her, throwing her off balance and letting her sink into the dense layer of black mud.

She tried to move and free herself, but her body became paralysed again, and her mouth was sealed shut. Without movement and voice, she had been reduced to pure consciousness inside a pool of darkness. The bitter liquid entered her mouth and thickly ran down her throat, suffocating the lungs. She was drowning. It wasn't until all but her eyes were under the sticky tar that Whalina saw a light figure.

The woman had the most beautiful arrangement of different shades of golden hair and wore a long, light pink dress. The angel-like creature floated towards Whalina with a smile that could break down a thousand rocks and deep blue eyes which would turn the ocean waters jealous. She penetrated the dry surface of the gunky sludge with her hands, and the concrete liquid transformed into water so clear that at last Whalina could see her reflection. Knee high in a pool of crystal-clear water, she found herself in a bubble of light her saviour had created.

"I have been waiting for you." Her voice was soft, making Whalina's heart beat faster with a familiar feeling of déjà vu.

She could not find the words, but her heart knew what the woman was about to tell her was something she already knew but had forgotten, like watching a film one knows the ending to, only that she was the main character.

"You are running out of time. You must come home at once." She reached for Whalina and pulled her to her feet.

"What home?" Whalina asked quietly, unsure if she could interrupt the goddess.

"Surely, you now understand why your painting could not be completed?" The woman's eyes widened in awe as Whalina's face revealed her confusion.

"So, it is true. You really have forgotten." The blazing light around the woman waned.

"I didn't mean to upset you. I just …" Whalina did not know what to say, feeling a cocktail of emotions in the pit of her stomach, making her nauseated with words.

"You are our last hope. Without you, there will be no tomorrow, and we will all cease to …" Her voice became softer until Whalina could hear no more.

Darkness crept around them again, for even the angel's bright light could not keep away the shadows. Whalina closed her eyes and allowed the darkness to consume her.

*****

Whalina awoke with a heavy weight on her chest. Her lungs felt like they were being tightened with coarse rope, and with each breath, the knot tightened. Her eyes opened with panic and scanned the foreign room for signs of danger. Surrounded by cream walls, she took no notice of the flowers or the leather chair next to the bed. She didn't see the bedside table and bag on the cold industrialised floor. She was lying in a hospital bed, covered with white sheets, in a room lacking life and colour.

Realising the person she most needed was not here, she heard the increased beeping on the heart monitor, confirming her existence. She was angry at God. Why had he let her live and not him? Wasn't God meant to be all-knowing and powerful? Didn't he know Neal was her world, that she didn't know how to be without him? Whalina opened her mouth to scream, but all that came out was a small, insignificant shriek. Prickly cacti needles pinched her throat as she swallowed.

The sound of the opening door grabbed her attention, and she thought she must be hallucinating. Someone who looked like her Neal walked through the door, holding a fluffy brown bear.

"Ali, you're awake." He wrapped his strong arms around her fragile body.

Whalina inhaled deeply. He smelt of sandalwood. He smelt like Neal. She didn't want to let him go, afraid he was a dream and that the veil of illusion could be lifted at any moment. The trickle of her warm tears mixed with his on her chest, and she knew he was real. Showered with a fusion of emotions and the relief that by some miracle they were both alive, they stayed silent, not letting go, until Neal gently caressed her face, wiping the tears off her pale cheeks.

Whalina's brain was rusty, struggling to pull words together that could express how she felt.

"I thought you ..." The words got stuck in her throat again.

"Died?"

Whalina could vividly remember seeing the paramedics leaning over his body, saving his life. With hundreds of questions coming to the surface, she whispered the most important one, "How are we both alive, Neal?"

"Do you remember what … happened?"

"I tried to keep my eyes open, to stay with you." Whalina recalled when, in the car, she had thought they had pulled the death card and were left to die.

"But then I found the strength to open my eyes, and I kicked the front window. The glass shattered into a million pieces, and then …" She paused, for she was unsure whether it had been all a dream. "There was a moment when I didn't feel the pressure inside my lungs, and I took the first chance I got and pulled you out." Saying it out loud did not make her feel any less crazy.

Whalina remembered her lungs burning and finally giving out. She had taken a deep breath underwater and released Neal's hand. She had thought it was the end, only it hadn't been, for she had opened her eyes and regained consciousness. Her mind had been sharp, without distractions, just a clear focus. She had pulled Neal to the shore, and that was where her memory became blurry.

"It was like I was given a new set of lungs and just enough oxygen to get us out." She wanted to continue, but a man with a blue tie and a stethoscope around his neck entered the room.

"Hello, Whalina. I'm Doctor Christofini. Glad to see you're back with us. How are you feeling?" The doctor put the stethoscope into his ears.

"What happened to me?" Her attention shifted to the sore leg muscles and the purple arm bruises.

The doctor patiently explained they had induced a coma to prevent swelling in the brain. He used medical jargon that went right over Whalina's head to explain the biological effects of drowning and that she would have to stay in the hospital for a few more days.

"May I listen to your chest, please?" He waited for her to nod before placing the cold diaphragm on her skin. After a few moments of carefully listening to her chest, he pulled away, shaking his head in disbelief.

"Absolute miracle, your lungs sound just fine," he said, smiling.

Whalina knew she should be grateful to even be alive, but the need to know and understand was overwhelming.

"I remember standing next to Neal, watching the paramedics save his life. I was conscious." She was aware of how crazy the words sounded out loud and began doubting herself.

"I'm afraid you were the unconscious one, Whalina. Please try not to worry about this right now. It's not uncommon to be a little disoriented. Things will soon make sense."

Before she could respond, his pager rang, and he left the room. Whalina was lost in a web of thoughts making her feel numb, as though a thick fog occupied her head and she could no longer be sure of anything.

"Ali, it's true," Neal said, as though he had read her mind. "You were unconscious. I have never been so afraid in my life as when your heart stopped beating." His voice was trembling. He took Whalina's hand into his and kissed it softly. "I'm never letting you go," he repeatedly said, clasping her hand inside his.

The comfort of his skin made her feel safe, and his presence was enough to help her mind relax.

"I was on the other side," she murmured, hoping it was clear enough for him to hear. She surrendered to the sound of his soft voice, without knowing when she had given in, and drifted into a deep sleep.

Chapter 3

The Signs All Around Us

After what seemed to be the longest four days of her life, Whalina was discharged. Longing for the promise of an ordinary life again, she pushed aside intruding thoughts of the accident and the things that could not be understood. It was easier to pretend everything was just fine, to lie to others and to herself. Her memories were still incoherently distorted, and she could not confront the possibility that she had breathed underwater, died, then came back to life.

Whalina convinced herself that she had not drowned but simply had waited for the car pressure to stabilise until she attempted to kick out the window. She was qualified in first aid, and it made sense that she had saved Neal's life by performing CPR. Once he had started breathing again, she must have passed out from exhaustion and the trauma of the accident. The doctors did not know why her heart had stopped beating, but as long as everything was fine now, the past was better left in the past.

*****

They lived on the third floor of a modern apartment block in Richmond. The area was known to be one of the most affluent spots in the city, filled with independent boutiques, bakeries, chic coffee shops, and organic food stores—an attractive place for tourists who often strolled by the riverside or visited one of the local historic pubs for a Sunday roast. Coming from the countryside, Whalina was not a fan of the fast-paced city life and tolerated it at best.

After graduating, she had moved to London for its cosmopolitan spirit and the array of job opportunities. It was a hub for many international creative companies and easy for a visionary brain like hers to find a job that paid well and that she hoped would also fulfil her dreams. Sacrificing the thriving country fields and the smell of freshly cut grass for a junior illustrator position seemed like the best option for a new graduate. Falling into the trap of the monotonous system of working long hours and looking forward to the weekend, Whalina had no chance to pause and ask herself if this was the life she truly wanted.

Growing up, she had aspired to become the next Picasso. From a young age, she held the paintbrush as though she had been painting for decades, and her parents always wondered from whom their daughter had inherited the talent. She would paint landscapes of places she had never visited, some real from photographs and some created in the jungle of infinite possibilities and worlds that existed in her fruitful visionary intellect. Around the age of twelve, she had vowed to one day own her own art gallery, yet, as with most adults, the reality of life had taken over, leaving no space for their childhood dreams in the harsh grown-up world. Drawing storyboards for an advertisement company was not exactly the art gallery she had hoped for, but still a private gallery she had.

Entering her apartment, Whalina felt relief to see the familiar inner world of her imagination framed on the walls. It was her happy place. Each room had a distinctive theme. The hallway showcased several abstract paintings, many of which represented the cosmos, featuring all sorts of swirls and spirals, whereas the living room was a display of wild animals, most of which were lions and whales. Her favourite painting hung in the bedroom—the rarest but equally beautiful world of unspoiled evergreen land; a diverse showcase of different shades of green, a surreal composition of dark and light shadows, with the most innocent of all blue skies providing an unparalleled contrast to the rich and transcendent woodland. Framed to the left was a narrow valley, curving supremely around the bold trees and a small footpath made of white marble rocks to its right.

The vivid, lucid world was what Whalina envisioned Heaven would be like. She thought the sublime air would permit her to take just one deep breath per day and that gravity would be of no concern, allowing her to jump over the valley and towards the great white

pieces together before; everything had a medical explanation, and it all just had to make sense.

"None of it is real, you silly girl," she said out loud as a sudden hot flush and intense thirst overcame her. She pulled herself up from the steaming water and opened her eyes, noticing all seven candles had been extinguished. Slowly scanning the obscure, steam-filled dark room, Whalina's heart raced, as she had never been a fan of the dark. Wrapped in a towel, she crept across the cold bathroom tiles and peeked her head across the long hallway.

She was about to step forward, but the harsh sound of the front door automatically closing pushed her body back inside the bathroom. Whalina quickly tried to reach for her phone on the bathtub's edge, but her shaking wet hands let the phone slip through and fall into the water-filled tub. Bent over the tub, she frantically searched for the phone under the surface of the artificial bubbles.

"Ali!"

She gasped, hearing her name, and burst into thick tears of raw emotion seeing Neal at the door, "I'm so-rry …"

"Shh. It's all right, it's all right." Neal wrapped his arms around her. He picked her up as one would a child and carried her to the bedroom, cradling her close as she woefully cried heavy tears she did not yet understand.

"Ali, talk to me. What's going on inside that beautiful mind of yours?" He guided Whalina's head from his chest so he could see her.

She tried to talk, but the words were muffled beyond comprehension.

"I'm really sorry about how I acted before." Neal lightly stroked her head. "I went to look for you, but you ran so fast."

The river of tears finally ran dry, and Whalina regained her voice.

"It's not you. My mind is just playing games with me."

"Tell me about the games, and we can play them together." His soft smile made her feel more at ease, and she tried to smile.

Whalina was unsure of where to begin her story, whether it was truly relevant to discuss the vision of the other world, or perhaps it was better to start with the raindrops on the windowsill.

"Hey, do you want to maybe paint tonight? That always helps you unwind." Neal's face brightened momentarily, and something clicked for Whalina.

"She was real. She must have been real. She knew about my painting," Whalina burst out and witnessed the internal workings of the neural pathways of her brain as she suddenly understood. Blossoming with a wide smile, she radiated confidence and shared the intimate details of her vision with Neal, from the moment that darkness had swallowed her down the vacuum hole, choked and filled her lungs with his thick black tar, and how the saviour had saved her life and brought her back to Earth.

"I know it sounds bizarre, fantasy at best. I know, Neal. But she mentioned the one painting I could never finish. She knew about my soulless woman painting. It's at my parents' house, and I need to find it. You do believe me, don't you?" Her eyes filled with the excitement of a child.

Neal silently watched her, and the fear of being judged surfaced.

"Yes, Ali, if you believe it, then so do I. Do you think it was your grandmother, or someone else like that?"

"I don't know. I really don't, but I'm just glad I have some kind of proof that I didn't imagine it all. I thought I was going crazy." And with that conclusion, Whalina rang her parents and arranged to visit for dinner tomorrow evening.

At last, the quiet night she so needed had arrived—a homemade meal and an early night in the arms of the one she loved the most. Exhausted by the emotional upheavals of the day, she quickly fell asleep, listening to the soft raindrops on the windowsill. That night, she travelled into a world her subconscious knew all too well. Her dream was of a baby whale, who swam by the side of its mother, belonging to the ocean and the ocean belonging to it. This is what love is truly about, being part of something greater than the self but remaining free and in your own essence. The whale allowed her to experience a place that came without question, a place within all beings, a place always waiting for you. Embodying the free spirit of the largest animal on the planet, she felt home. Dreams are very much like real life, in that they take us in directions we could never see coming.

Without warning, Whalina was stripped of her whale body, becoming a separate entity, and was pulled into its gigantic mouth. Her eyes fixated on the tiny light at the opening of its mouth that grew smaller as she slid down its tongue into infinite darkness. Whalina choked and gagged at the stench of rotting fish and her heart pounded all the way up to her throat. Opening her mouth wide, begging to be heard, she found herself muted and abandoned in the colossal space.

Oppressed by the heavy stomach walls, convinced all efforts were futile and that this was the end, she gave up. Only then, by some miracle, she was sucked into the whale's blowhole and emerged covered in sticky mucus. The dream ended, waking her up gasping for air.

CHAPTER 4

THE BLUE PATH

Time: Nine months before Whalina's birth
Location: Utopian land of the Kingdom of Light

> *The ocean is the most spectacular show in the whole universe. It is an endless flow, representing the consciousness that lives inside us all. It is a never-ending journey that has been unfolding since the beginning of time. It continues to create a never-ending story of waves that fold and fall apart, unapologetically knowing they will rise again, or so Mother Nature had planned.*

When Remedy opened the shiny satin curtains that fine morning, she expected a gentle breeze to brush over her skin, but instead, she was met with arid, hot air. Even in the early hours, the deep-red sun was blazing. It would be yet another hot day, and Remedy had had enough of hot days. The tall tower window overlooked the vast calm water, and, for a moment, Remedy stood motionless, the stillness of the ocean mesmerizing her. She thought about how much she would love to jump in and have its coolness engulf her. The ocean had always been her cocoon; she was its butterfly, safe and sound, feeling light as a feather supported by the dense saltwater.

Looking over the eternal sea, she smiled wholeheartedly. Every time she saw the land's sublime beauty, she felt grateful for being one of its guardians. Not just any land, but one of the oldest kingdoms in the universe, far more superior and advanced than Earth. Yet, that wasn't how Remedy would describe the Kingdom of Light. She saw the goodness inside the hearts of its people and the overarching desire to be good and do good. That very desire was a rare occurrence on Earth, making this place one of a kind. The oceans here were free from pollution and fishing. Hunting and murder were unheard of. People lived off on what the land gave them, and because the land was looked after, there was always more than enough of everything that a pure human heart could possibly desire. A definite glow alit the faces of the people who walked this land, a light so bright that made the existence of darkness difficult, if not impossible. Elsewhere, in past lifetimes, the people here had endured their fair share of pain and heartbreak and had evolved beyond all that now, making Earth an inhabitable place for such souls.

Whilst overlooking the rich landscape filled with green forests, mountains, and the ocean, Remedy braided her long golden hair and tied it neatly with a blue ribbon at the end. She was about to turn her back to the window when Jupiter appeared flapping a gush of warm air into the room with his giant wings and catching Remedy off guard.

"Jupiter, you're back!" She scratched behind her flying lion's big, fluffy ear. Jupiter's furry mane resembled the bright sun behind him. Without hesitation, Remedy stood on the windowsill and carefully swung her leg over the grand cat, sitting comfortably on its back. *Ready!*

The air, the girl, and her lion become one as they soared together through the cloudless sky. Defying the rules of gravity and floating effortlessly on the supportive air was one of Remedy's favourite pastimes. The freedom she experienced could be compared to a stallion galloping with the wind. Each member of the guardian family was gifted with a spirit animal. The animal would often appear at unexpected times but always with a purpose. Jupiter's visits were an adventure to Remedy; they meant change or challenge was on its way, and her lion was here to remind her that whatever was coming her way, she would never be alone.

Beholding the kingdom and the beautiful planet she belonged to always shifted her perspective to one of gratitude and serenity. Suddenly, she didn't mind the scorching sun but appreciated all it did for the kingdom. Looking down, Remedy took in the endless life and colour beneath them.

Fresh fruits and vegetables blossomed on the corner of every street, supplying an abundance of health and vitality to the kingdom's residents. Nature had completely eradicated the world hunger problem Earth had been battling for millennia. People took care of the land, so the land took care of them. The streets were named after the food source that grew in the area; Almando Road was known for its supply of almonds, and Egvile was where the wild chickens resided. The enlightened chickens knew to separate their fertilised eggs from the ones they could spare for the people. Unlike Earth, readily available cow's milk did not exist. Certainly, cows roamed the land, but they did so freely, grazing in the greenest of fields, celebrated by the humans. They would dress them in handmade marigold necklaces, massage their backs, and occasionally, a cow would pick herself a human friend whom she would share her precious milk. Indeed, people had come a long way since their Earthly existence. Their souls had enough time and lives to not only learn but to deeply engrave into their being, love and respect for all.

As they flew over Bagel Street, the smell of freshly baked bread rose through the warm air, reminding Remedy of the breakfast plans she had made with her grandmother. *Let's go back home.*

Jupiter changed course and glided towards the palace gardens.

Remedy turned back one last time to look at the ocean and how unbelievably still it was. From above, it appeared as though a cloak had been placed over the surface, and the thought of being able to walk on water crossed Remedy's mind. Certain that her eyes were playing tricks on her, she focused on the garden's crystal lake and spotted the short, grey-haired woman waving to her.

Jupiter descended quickly and made a smooth landing just by the red apple tree.

Before jumping off, Remedy picked the two ripest fruits off the tree. "Gran," she said, hugging the elderly woman. "I lost track of time. I hope you weren't waiting too long." Remedy placed the two apples on the fruit tray her grandmother had prepared.

"I don't mind waiting, but you might have upset the cherries." She giggled, letting her youthful soul shine through.

Remedy smiled and sat on the vibrant green grass by the clear lake. The cherries did look a little sad. Their once-perky skin was wrinkled, and their usual bright red colour was shy of pink. "That's unusual. I understand cherries are a sensitive fruit, but to get distressed because they weren't eaten right away, that's a little dramatic even for them," Remedy said with a mouthful of small cherries.

"All that grows, grows for us, and once picked and ripped from the soil, must be eaten in a timely manner, sweet child."

Of course, Remedy knew that but still thought the cherries were a little too emotional today. Perhaps it was the approaching full moon; it had a way of affecting one's mood.

Remedy's grandmother Sacnicte was one of the kingdom's eldest and most respected people. She had discovered her soul's purpose at a very young age and knew why she had been reincarnated to live in the kingdom. The kingdom existed as a union, but, as with all unions, there was some individualism, so people still held their own life paths that collectively worked together. Sacnicte had been born with an extraordinary gift that helped others find the road that would lead them to discover their purpose.

One essential group of people who Sacnicte helped were the Lightworkers—a special group of wise souls who had descended to Earth to help raise the consciousness of humanity. They were born to inspire positive movement and change amongst the population. Once their work was complete, they would die and return to the kingdom or travel to higher dimensions. The ones who returned knew their purpose was not yet complete and would return to Earth's trenches once again. Sacnicte helped to rehabilitate the souls who had returned from Earth and counsel them through their experiences so they could return to finish their work. Once on Earth, the Lightworkers did not remember why they came, nor did they know their true power. In fact, they would often refer to themselves as 'old souls,' knowing they had been on Earth before yet not fully understanding why they had returned.

"Have you finished your painting, Remi?" Sacnicte tossed a cherry into her mouth and spat it out right away. "They are spoiled throughout. How strange." The old woman placed the blushing cherries on the grass, knowing they would decompose and be transformed into new life soon again.

Remedy appreciated the extra moment she had to think of an answer. "I'm getting closer," she said, looking into the distance of the nearby forest, hoping to find something she could distract her grandmother with.

"I'm sensing disappointment, Remi." Sacnicte took the petite hand into hers. The eyes which had once been the colour of the ocean were now merely a washed steel shade of blue, reflected in her granddaughter's turquoise eyes. The kind eyes and curve of the wrinkled skin around her lips softened Remedy's rigid expectations of herself.

"I know patience is not my greatest virtue, but I'm nearly eighteen, and I thought my life purpose would become clear by now." She sighed, placing the warm bread on the plate.

One's life purpose usually revealed itself before the eighteenth birthday, and Remedy was seven days short of the big day. The life purpose of those residing in the Kingdom of Light was no way different from those on Earth. They varied in what needed to be learnt and experienced to become a more evolved and expansive soul.

"I need to know why the gods have given me another life. How can I serve my people if I don't know what I'm meant to be doing?" Remedy looked straight into her grandmother's eyes, searching for answers, but before the old woman opened her mouth, Remedy continued, "When you were my age, you were guiding thousands of Lightworkers to Earth. You were a leader, and I always hoped someday I, too, could match your gift to humanity." She paused, taking in the softness of her grandmother's face. Her kind eyes centred her into speaking her truth. "I am full of gratitude for my life, I am, but it's all becoming meaningless. I wake up and go to sleep every night without making a difference in the world. I don't feel like a guardian, Grandma. I'm just an ordinary girl who is searching for something that could make her special."

A deep sadness spread across her heart as the sound of the words made the feeling more real. Whether Remedy was aware of it or not, Sacnicte's gift worked miracles on her. Everything she had ever said, thought, and experienced had led her to this very moment, and all for good reason.

"Ever thought that perhaps it's the world that is not yet ready for your gift?" Sacnicte didn't need much time to formulate a response. Remedy knew there was more, as she waited patiently for her grandmother to finish what she had started. A gentle crease formulated between the old woman's eyes, matching Remedy's tight eyebrows. "All the answers are already inside you, Remi. Your struggle at finishing the painting is not the problem, but your lack of trust in yourself and your intuition *is*. Your heart is your greatest source of wisdom." Sacnicte spoke in a gentle tone, which Remedy knew very well. Her grandmother always lowered her voice when the content of her words was of particular importance. It was a conscious way of ensuring that one was paying attention by working their ears a little harder to hear the soft voice. "Use it," she finished and took a bite from the juicy apple.

Deep down, Remedy knew her grandmother was right. She had first begun sketching the painting over two years ago. It was a self-portrait which was supposed to fuel her creativity and help her reach a deeper understanding of her purpose and who she was. Yet every time she was close to its completion, she changed her mind about the colour of her soul. The shading around her heart never felt *just right,* so she would start again, driving herself mad, trying time and again. She became obsessed with the final image, the destination, and forgot to enjoy the journey.

"I guess you might be right, Gran. Perhaps I should relax about the painting and trust that when the time's right, I'll know what to do," Remedy said, half believing her own words.

She could hear her grandmother's voice run to the back of her head when, suddenly, the mesmerising water of the turquoise lake made it impossible to translate Sacnicte's words into comprehensible meaning. What her eyes could see was much more interesting than the wise woman's words. The water was inviting, the surface asking to be broken, to be touched. Remedy gave in. Yearning to be the one to break the stillness, she reached for the surface, when Sacnicte broke the invisible spell and grabbed her hand.

"I have to say, you're acting more peculiar than usual. I have something to show you. Come." She walked away, making Remedy quickly jump to her feet.

The palace was home to the eldest and most beautiful gardens in the kingdom. A kingdom guardian, from several generations before, had immaculately arranged hundreds of different flowers and plant species. But today, edible vegetation, flowers, bushes, ancient trees, and even a garden labyrinth now filled the three hundred acres of land. As it happened, the role of the garden caretaker was passed down to the eldest woman of the family. Sacnicte had been caring for the gardens since her mother had passed, some twenty years before.

Remedy wrapped her arm around her grandmother's as they silently walked over the cool, green grass. To the right lay a charming array of the most delicate red roses. Sacnicte said they were a cherry shade of red, but to Remedy, they looked candy red.

When the gentle wind blew, carrying the fresh smell of the flowers, Remedy exclaimed, "They smell like candy, they look like candy. Grandma, these are rose-flavoured candies!" She ran to the rose bush and touched the petals.

One by one, they fell off the rose head and into her hands and turned into small red candy. Carrying a big grin, Remedy approached Sacnicte and shared the sweets. "I guess it is candy red after all, Gran." She bit hard to crush the candy.

"They are whatever you want them to be." Sacnicte opened her hand to reveal a handful of cherries. "Remember, this garden was created in my mind's eye. My energy is intertwined in every underground root and every leaf under the sun."

"So, if the garden sees you as its creator, why did the rose respond to me and turn into candy?"

"Because you are your own creator, dear. When you combined your thoughts with the elevated emotion of excitement, you turned energy into motion, or roses into candy," Sacnicte finished, satisfying her granddaughter's curiosity for a moment.

This was one of the main fundamental differences between what happened on Earth and how the Light habitants responded to life. Humans have the same power to create with their brilliant minds and emotions, transforming concepts into matter. Airplanes had not been created from thin air; someone had thought about the idea first. They had imagined the feeling of soaring at nine hundred kilometres per hour and combined it with the possibility of a machinelike vessel that could make it happen. Of course, a lot more work goes into making an idea come to fruition, but all that exists on Earth or in any dimension had to be thought of first and created second. Yet too often humans attribute their blessings and miracles to luck, someone else's kindness, or perhaps their misfortune. Rarely do they stop and acknowledge their own power and believe they, too, can physically manifest things they wish to happen.

The only difference was the Light habitants knew their power, and when Remedy turned the rose into candy, it didn't come as a surprise, because it wasn't the first time something extraordinary had happened. The first time Remedy had witnessed a grand miracle was when she was nine years old. The kingdom had been in desperate need of water. It hadn't rained for over three months, food reserves were running low, and wildlife was pleading for help. Remedy's parents, the head guardians of the kingdom, had asked all Light habitants to gather outside their houses and hold hands. They had worked in unison for a whole day, and by sunset, they had formed a bond that began right by the sea and continued all the way up to the palace, and together they had thought of rain. They had visualised warm water pouring from the sky, wet hair, and soaking clothes. Shoes had filled with water, soil had become moist, and the sound of children playing in puddles had permeated the air. They had imagined the taste of rainwater on their tongues and the joy the rain would bring. Their hearts had expanded with gratitude, as though it had already happened, and just before sunrise, it had begun to rain. From that day onwards, Remedy knew nothing was impossible and that she should never underestimate the power of her thoughts.

Sacnicte gently pulled her granddaughter to the left. The new path had a different type of energy; it was no place for the creation of candy nor cherries. A cocktail of lavender and blue chrysanthemums bracketed both sides of the path. It was difficult to separate one from the other, and a tall, ancient tree did a great job blocking the sunlight.

Noticing a drop in temperature, Remedy rolled down her sleeves. "I don't think I've ever been to this part of the garden, Gran. What is this place?" Her big blue eyes looked even bigger as she stared wide-eyed at everything around her.

"That's right, child. Your parents are the only other people who know about this place." Sacnicte loosened her hold on Remedy's arm.

"Ready to bloom, aren't you?" she said to the bell-shaped white flowers hanging upside down from the small branches of the bush. Curious to see and smell the inside of the flower, Remedy bent down and began to reach for the plant but felt her grandmother's small but strong hands on her shoulders.

"No. Don't touch, and certainly don't smell," she spoke directly to Remedy's soul through her eyes.

The two women, two generations apart, stood in front of the plant.

"I am preparing for a journey in search of answers that can be found in a different dimension. These plants will help me get there." Sacnicte's voice turned soft again.

Remedy had questions of her own. She remembered her mother warning her against those flowers when she was just a child, saying, *"If you come across the upside-down bell, come home right away or you might never return again."*

"Grandma, but how will you return?" she asked whilst fixating on the flower.

"I can find my way back, child. In three days, they will be ready to harvest. Can I count on your help?" Sacnicte was now whispering.

"Of course. Anything you need, Grandma," Remedy whispered and walked shortly behind Sacnicte across the blue-flowered path. She looked behind at the upside-down bells and her mind filled with questions, yet she knew better than to quiz her grandmother.

When they exited the darkened path and shade, the blazing sun hit their faces, and the humid air entered their lungs. It was going to be an insufferable day, and they sought relief at the lake, where they had left their breakfast picnic some time ago. The red apples, bread, and fresh garden salad sweetened with pomegranate seeds had been waiting. They sat and ate, exchanging only a few words between their bites. Remedy was deeply engrossed at the idea of travelling to a different realm and wondered what kind of questions her grandmother had.

"I would prefer if you could keep the conversation we had on the blue path to yourself, please," Sacnicte said, placing her feet in the lake water.

"Yes, of course, Grandma. But can I just ask, is the kingdom in some kind of danger?" She watched Sacnicte's wrinkled face turn pale. "Grandma, what's going on?" She scooted closer and kneeled by the old lady.

Sacnicte was trying to speak, but something had a hold of her tongue.

"Talk to me. What can I do?" Remedy shouted and grabbed the cup of water her grandmother had been drinking.

Sacnicte could not swallow and spat the water onto her embroidered white dress, leaving light-pink stains. "He is back." Sacnicte spoke slowly and ever so softly.

"Who? Who is back, Grandma?" Remedy fought back her tears whilst holding her grandmother's head in her hands.

"Remedy, you are the saviour." Blood spilled from her mouth as she gasped for air. "Not my choice to die. Don't trust ..." Sacnicte's gaze gripped onto her granddaughter, and although Remedy wanted to shout for help, she knew in her gut that it was not what her grandmother needed.

Without wasting another precious second, she gently tucked the frail, grey hair blowing with the wind behind her ears. "Grandma, please don't leave me. Please, I need you," she pleaded as tears rolled down her cheeks and fell onto her grandmother's face. Remedy knew this was the end, but, for a moment longer, she wanted to believe it wasn't. She wanted to grab time by its neck and shout, *"Stop! I'm not ready to let go!"* but even she could not come between the relationship that death and time shared.

It had all happened so quickly; one moment they were laughing about spoiled cherries, walking down the blue path, and the next she was holding her grandmother through her last breath. She felt as though time was stolen from her, so many questions unanswered and memories that could never be again. With all her heart, Remedy wanted to know her purpose and to share it with her grandmother, but now all of that and much more was lost.

Sacnicte's eyes changed colour. The blue faded, telling the truth of what her heart felt. Remedy knew it was time. Soft lines formed around Sacnicte's mouth as her lips curved into a smile for the last time.

"I believe in you," were the final words Remedy heard her grandmother say. The last blue in her eyes turned white as her soul left the body.

CHAPTER 5

THE LAST JOURNEY WITH THE SUN

Time: Nine Month Before Whalina's Birth
Location: Falling Land of the Kingdom of Light

"Papa, Papa!" Remedy shouted at the top of her lungs. Sacnicte's chest was no longer rising, and Remedy was holding onto her last bit of strength as she tried to resuscitate the heart. It seemed that no matter how much Remedy wanted to bring her grandmother back to life, Sacnicte would not start to breathe.

It came as a surprise when Papa's big and firm hands pulled her from the dead body. "Darling, it's enough. Your grandmother is not here," he said intently and pulled her into his arms.

"She didn't want to die. She wasn't ready," she muffled through the ocean of tears. Cradled by the warmth of her father, Remedy could hear her heart racing, and just for a moment, she imagined it stopping so she too could leave and go wherever her grandmother had gone. Knowing the immense power of her mind, she pushed the thought away and looked up into Papa's brown eyes. Something seemed alien about them, and Remedy could not tell what her father was thinking. "Papa, what's wrong?"

Papa pulled her closer, and although she could not see his smile, she thought she could hear it—Papa's lips cracking, a small exhalation that could be a laugh. He held her tightly, and finally, she surrendered to a sudden wave of sleep.

*****

ing, also dressed in white. Little was said as they walked through the grand salon on the cold marble floor.

"Chin up, Remi. This is a celebration of life," Papa said, and Remedy could not believe the joy on his face.

Sacnicte's death looked like murder rather than a much-wanted opportunity for rebirth. Remedy could not understand why her parents were so accepting of what had happened. For centuries, those who were about to pass to a new dimension would give warning to their loved ones, who would arrange a proper goodbye ceremony. Sacnicte had not given warning, which Remedy felt in her gut was a sign of something about to go wrong.

The three of them walked barefoot down the silent garden. Remedy shared her grief with the silence of the birds and animals, who usually roamed freely through the land. The sweet sound of singing sparrows grew louder as they approached the entrance to the red forest of Adamah, where Sacnicte awaited them. Donning a one-of-a-kind dress created purely from fresh white and purple lilies, she lay on a bed made from bamboo.

"Go ahead, Remedy," Mama encouraged her as Remedy approached her grandmother and wondered where the other bloodstained dress had gone.

Sacnicte looked the same as she had that morning, yet different. Her face appeared fuller and rounder, and when Remedy leaned in to hug her, she didn't smell like her grandmother. Instead of the usual floral, earthy smell, Sacnicte reminded her of something artificial, like her grandmother was made to look and smell pretty. Yet, she was so much more than that. The unreciprocated hug was cool, and where once a heart full of love and life used to be was eternal stillness. Remedy recoiled and wished she hadn't gone near what remained of her beloved grandmother. The cold embrace tainted the warm memory of Sacnicte's benevolent energy, and Remedy desperately wanted to be anywhere but here.

Papa was next, and he remained indifferent as he cradled his mother in his arms. Mama refrained from hugging all together and simply held Sacnicte's hand for a moment. Remedy watched the palace attendants hoist the bamboo bed and walk to Sacnicte's burial tree, the Giant Sequoia. Its trunk was about nine metres thick, and a small hollow hole had been carved out on one side. In comparison to the thirty-foot-tall tree, the hole was small yet large enough to accommodate Sacnicte's body, which the attendants lifted with great care inside the embrace of the majestic tree.

"She looks so small, Ma," Remedy whispered.

"By tomorrow, your grandmother will be in another world." Ma squeezed Remedy's hand.

The sun was believed to carry the soul to the next phase of existence. Once the heart stopped beating, the burial had to take place at the very next sunset. By sunrise the next day, Sacnicte's body would turn into ash, and her soul would be someplace nobody knew, and what would remain was what she had created whilst alive. The gardens would persevere to grow, and the hearts of the people she had touched whilst living would continue with their purpose.

The attendants created a fire a few feet from Sacnicte's tree. They carried two large wooden crates filled with her personal belongings. Inside, amongst other miscellaneous items, were clothes, books, paintings she had both painted and had been gifted, and her favourite cooking spices and herbs.

"Ma, what are they doing with Grandma's stuff?" Remedy panicked. It couldn't possibly be what she thought it was.

"Remi, come forward please," Papa said, and Remedy no longer needed Mama to answer the question, for she understood. "Take an item from one of the boxes, and when you feel ready, release it into the fire."

Every bone in Remedy's body was fighting her. Sacnicte's belongings were all that she had left of her grandmother.

"Papa, please, can I keep something?" she asked with faith that an exception could be made for her, just this once. She had, of course, read about burials and logically understood why things happened the way they did, but being the one on the frontline, experiencing the burial first hand was entirely different. Although her mind understood, her heart was bewildered.

"Your grandmother's energy no longer belongs here, Remi. We must not remain attached to what is no longer real," he said with no emotion behind his eyes. Remedy had never seen her Papa behave this way. He was always so warm, understanding, and in many ways, he was her teacher and role model.

Overcome by confusion and grief, Remedy had no fight left in her, and when she placed her hand in the large container, she picked up the first piece of clothing that came into her hands. It was a silky, rose-coloured velvet dress, and between the fabric was a hard, cool circular object. As she unfolded the dress, a golden ring with a shiny purple stone appeared. Remedy stowed the ring under her sleeve, and with a heavy heart, she let the dress slip through her fingers, and the wind pulled it into the fire. She gripped the ring and returned to stand alongside Mama whilst the attendants placed the wooden crates into the fire.

Remedy felt as though a piece of herself was in the fire too, and her insides were about to explode. As though chains had been wrapped around her chest, pressure was forming, suffocating her throat. It felt like a ball of cotton was stuck down her windpipe, making each breath more brutal than the last.

Remedy studied her grandmother, knowing this would be the final time she'd ever see her, and whispered, "I won't let you down." Swallowing her tears, she could no longer watch Sacnicte's lifetime of belongings burn to the ground. She had to leave. The horizon had finally swallowed the sun, and Remedy released Mama's hand to return to the dark forest.

Unsure why or when she started, Remedy ran faster than ever.

CHAPTER 6

THE TIME TRAP

The gentle sunrays were peeking into the bedroom when a loud noise disturbed the harmony of the morning birdsong. It took Whalina some time to become conscious and awake enough to answer the ringing phone. She strode to the kitchen and stood next to the calendar whilst she apologised, acknowledging that, indeed, it was the first of the month. Whalina always thought of Kate, the receptionist at the psychology clinic, as an unhappy person. Hearing her tired voice over the phone and how every task turned into an obstacle suggested that perhaps Kate could benefit from sessions with a therapist herself.

Whalina pleaded for another appointment, explaining that with the accident and all the aftermath, she had simply forgotten. After Whalina heard several sighs and groans on the other end of the phone, Kate offered what was apparently the only available slot for the rest of the month. Desperate to see her therapist, Whalina agreed, knowing she would have to leave the house immediately.

She swapped the T-shirt in which she had slept in for a white dress filled with vibrant sunflowers. With her hair in a messy ponytail, she brushed her teeth in half the time she usually needed and approved the five-minute look with a glance in the mirror. Whilst tying her white Converses, she thought of Neal and was surprised he was still sleeping. She held her breath to hear his and peeked through the ajar bedroom door to confirm that he was still, in fact, alive. It took a few seconds of concentration to hear his soft, almost inaudible breath. Before leaving, she wrote a note saying where she was going and stuck it to the fridge with a magnet they had bought together on their holiday

Whalina slipped off her shoes and sat under the lone tree. She heard him pouring the tea and smelled the refreshing Moroccan green-mint flavour.

Pedro placed the teapot on the glass table and sat opposite Whalina.

"Please help yourself."

Whalina responded by pouring the hot tea to the very top of her porcelain cup.

Pedro adjusted his glasses on his nose, and the clock facing him began the countdown.

Whalina summarised their trivial time in Cornwall and the physical overview of what had happened during the accident. Conscious of time, she highlighted the moments that had made the greatest impact—particularly the vision of the golden woman who had saved her life and the women's connection to the painting, which Whalina could not finish, no matter how many times she had tried—the feeling of suffocating inside her lungs, drowning, and saying goodbye to Neal yet surviving.

"I believe I have been given a second chance at life," she concluded whilst taking a sip of the refreshing tea.

"And how does that make you feel?" Pedro maintained eye contact.

"Grateful, of course, but there's also pressure to get it right, you know?" She sighed deeply. "I can no longer deny that I have all the time in the world. I'm here today and gone tomorrow." The illusion that life was eternal had burst for Whalina. Confronted with her mortality, Whalina knew time was more of an essence than ever before.

"And this painting, why is it so important that you complete it?" Pedro asked whilst scribbling something in his notepad.

Whalina did not know the answer. She didn't know why the painting mattered, only that it did. "I died. I'm pretty sure of it, and the woman who brought me back wanted me to finish the painting. I just know this is something I need to do." After another deep sigh, she continued, "I want to stop feeling empty inside. Stop thinking that for my life to matter, I need to do something big and grand to create change in the world and not be forgotten."

The sound of a scribbling pen filled the room as Pedro took a few more notes.

"And how will completing the painting help you feel significant?"

Whalina was once again unsure of the answer, and a part of her wished she had never told Pedro about the painting. He was doing his job, digging for answers in all the uncomfortable, painful places. "I want to finish what I started. It might not change anything, but I will feel better knowing it's finished," Whalina said, fully aware that what she was saying probably made no sense to her therapist. "I want to have a plan, a purpose, a reason for life," she needed to add.

"I'm speaking hypothetically here. If you were to die tomorrow, would you spend today worrying about tomorrow?"

It took a moment for Whalina to fully comprehend Pedro's question. "Of course not. I would want to live my best life today." The words did not feel untrue in her mouth.

"Every day is a race against time. There is so much I want to do, but who knows how much time I have left?" She stopped talking, feeling her heart flutter with vulnerability.

Whalina felt increasingly uneasy, unconsciously picking at the soft skin of her arm. Her mind was numb yet overflowing with thought, creating a trying pressure inside her brain, which wanted to shut down and work things through at the same time.

Pedro asked Whalina to close her eyes and lay down.

As instructed, she took five deep breaths, imagining her breath was like a wave in the ocean. On the inhale, her belly and chest would rise like the sea waves, and with the exhale, it would fall. The fresh spring air ran through her body, bringing a sense of calm.

"Please go back to your first memory of time. How did you feel? What did you do?" he asked in a slow, monotonous voice.

In her mind, a movie played about a teenager who was afraid to live, in case she missed life itself. So concerned with the passaging of time, birthdays, anniversaries, and holidays were nothing more than an inconvenience to share with the family. Hearing ABBA at her seventeenth birthday had triggered her in the worst of ways: suffocating her with the illogical conviction that the *"young and sweet, only seventeen dancing queen"* would not live another year. Whalina's fears had gotten the best of her, and after that evening, she had removed all the clocks, calendars, and watches in the house.

"And now, leave this memory, this era, and go to the next image," Pedro said, continuing to guide her in the hypnotic meditation.

The painting was the one that had stolen the most time in her youth—the painting that she loved and hated equally. Loved so much that she would begin anew on a fresh canvas each time, because something would seem dishonest or misguided with the previous one. The love mixed with hate for the frustration and unfulfilled ambition would keep her awake at night.

Whalina jumped to the next image of her skinny fingers pressing the piano keys. The memory was vivid in her head, as it was the day she had met Neal. Whilst she was lost in the melody, he had startled her as he entered the music room's practice space they shared at the university. She had immediately checked her watch. Before having a chance to talk to the boy, she had rushed to the door and lay in bed that night feeling both angry and sorry for herself. Whalina had felt drawn to Neal from the moment she saw him, but her rigid mind and fixation on time would not allow for a deviation from the schedule.

Whalina listened to Pedro's guiding voice, her mind jumped through a series of flashbacks, exposing the numerous times she had lost her temper when Neal was late. She saw his patience each time he had held her through a breakdown and panic. He believed her fear as though it was his own and not once made her feel different or crazy because of it. In fact, he had helped her embrace and love the shadows that lived beside her.

As Pedro continuously encouraged her to stay in the present moment, the past and future ceased to exist, and the only time that was real was the eternal now. Whalina came to a realisation. If tomorrow was an illusion and yesterday was a memory, then all that mattered was today, and if she died today, then the most noteworthy moment of her life was the one where she would draw her last breath.

Pedro gradually increased the volume of his voice, returning Whalina to the red-brick room. She took her time readapting and, when ready, sat crisscross on the sofa. She felt refreshed, as though she had just woken up after a long night's sleep.

"Would you like to share your experience?"

Whalina nodded in agreement. "It has never been about how long we live. It's about how we live today. The only time we have is now. Thank you, Pedro." She often wanted to hug him, but even after ten years of therapy, it was hardly appropriate.

"I think you've answered the question you came here with," the psychologist said with a sense of tranquillity and certainty in his eyes.

"There's something else I would like to get your opinion on," Whalina began whilst pouring the last of the remaining contents of the teapot into her cup. Being swallowed by a whale was hardly an encounter one could forget, even if it had been a dream. As best as her memory would serve her, she put together the disturbing imagery of the dream from the night before.

With one hand on his beard, Pedro thought for a moment. It was common for him to pause and think before he spoke, a quality that humanity could learn to appreciate and embody. "Do you know the story of Jonah and the whale?"

Whalina shook her head.

He told her the Old Testament story of the Israelite Jonah, whom God had chosen to be a prophet. Jonah refused his divine mission and left on a sea voyage instead. During a terrible storm, the sailors realised that Jonah's disobedience had caused the weather conditions, and to save their ship, they threw Jonah overboard. A huge fish swallowed the man, and for three days and nights, he prayed to God. He committed and promised to do what he was called to do. Hearing this, God commanded the whale to vomit Jonah out.

The clock in front of Pedro flashed brightly and displayed four zeros.

"All the answers to the asked and unasked questions are inside you, Whalina. I cannot tell you what your dream means. Only you can do that," he said, smiling.

"I need to embrace what is coming. I need to finish what I started," she said to herself, then asked Pedro, "Is my time over?" Her eyebrows naturally raised.

"Yes, this time in space is over," he answered, smiling from his wrinkled eyes.

Whalina left the room with a new sense of purpose, gratitude radiating from her smile. She thanked the receptionist for making the appointment possible, and her light presence seemed to even infect Kate, who looked rather pleased with herself.

On the way home, she briefly stopped to admire mama swan and her children. Whalina watched the youth of the cygnets, for soon, nine new swans—although born grey and fluffy would transform into one of the most majestic birds on Earth—would fill the lake. She contemplated how wonderful time was, in that it allowed for transformation and the creation of beauty. It allowed us to change, grow, and become someone new every day. Feeling blissful and full of wonder, Whalina knew what she needed to do next. Hoping the painting would still be there, she called her father and confirmed that she and Neal would see them for dinner later today.

CHAPTER 7

THE GREAT WORDS THAT ARE LEFT UNSAID

The train between London and Cambridge ran for just over an hour, yet usually the time seemed to pass much faster. Today, the journey felt drawn out as time slowed down for Whalina, who was becoming increasingly nervous about finding the lost paintings. Her session with Pedro earlier that morning seemed to have happened a lifetime ago, as a new adventure was beginning to unfold. Whalina found some comfort in the simplicity of holding Neal's hand as they gazed over the fast-changing evergreen countryside.

"I hope my parents won't freak out when I mention the painting," she said with unease, feeling the surface of her hand moisten with nerves.

"Ask your dad first," Neal suggested, and Whalina smiled back, knowing that had been the plan all along.

"You still didn't tell me what's so special about this one painting" he said quietly, and as she faced him, her eyes already told the sad story. "Forget I asked, Al. We still have over half an hour to go. Try to nap for a bit." He rolled his jumper into a pillow and placed it on his shoulder.

Whalina gathered the hair covering her face, tied the wild strands into a high bun, and folded her arms. "I think you should know," she said.

There was never a good time to exhume the skeletons she had kept buried for over a decade. The intention of completing the painting had turned into a torment that forever changed the way she viewed art. If it wasn't for that very painting, she'd have her own gallery by now;

instead, it was safer to draw storyboards, as the fear of losing her sanity was a risk she was unwilling to take.

A few days before her sixteenth birthday, she had created the first version of the painting, which would later have several copies. Until then, her art had mainly depicted animals and nature but very rarely people. Even then, it was people she knew—portraits of her parents and younger sister—yet she had undoubtedly pulled this feminine figure from pure imagination. She could not be traced back to a film, book, or magazine picture. One day, Whalina had simply awoken and began painting. Clearly remembering that day, as the ones that followed all merged into one, the young artist had painted all day, declining all offers of food and drink.

After several hours and past bedtime, a beautiful, naked female figure had stood facing forward at the centre of the canvas, head turned to the right, with luscious, long golden hair covering half of the body. The delicate hands and slender fingers crossed together and had been placed gracefully on the left hip. The small feet, crossed at the ankles, had toes buried into the ground. It was up to the eyes of the beholder to decide whether the being was descending and sinking into the soil or emerging from an earthy rebirth. The wide childbearing hips and defined muscles spoke of invincible femininity and warrior spirit. The sun-kissed hair covered nearly all her face except the eyes, and it was unclear whether the goddess was turning back or moving forward. The body translated into power, and although she had a kind face, her black eyes boasted a look that could kill with just a blink.

The background was sky blue, contrasting the dirt beneath the feet, and the only distraction from the woman was a stone bridge situated across the two edges of the frame. It was left to one's imagination to envision what the structure was providing a connection between. That had been the first of the many duplicates of the same painting, except for the background changing to different shades of blue. Young Whalina would stop painting in the exact same place each time. The depicted figure's skin was pale with a hint of a rosy tint, and colour covered the canvas, with only a small empty space in the middle of the warrior's chest. Finding the right pigmentation for this woman's soul had become an obsession occupying Whalina's imagination in the day and her dreams at night. Naturally, one would expect the soul of such a remarkable angel-like figure to be pure, innocent, and bright in colour. Yet something felt so wrong about depicting a living being in only one shade; surely there was more to her than the goddess; there was more that could be seen on the exterior. When the room had filled with several drafts of the same painting and the woman who had once defined ambition now represented an adverse compulsion, it had finally all ended.

"Mum forced me to go to Wales with her, and when I came back, all my paintings were gone."

The bedroom was free of all the eighteen paintings she had titled *The Soulless Woman*, and the opened curtains allowed fresh air to flow through, taking the idle concerns of a childish dilemma out the window.

"At first, I was furious, but eventually, I understood that perhaps it was for my own good. That was when I met Pedro." Whalina sounded unsure of herself, and the tone of her voice had swayed in another direction.

With the help of Dr Wood, the young girl had abandoned the search of finding the glow, the right colour fit for this divine soul, and stopped painting for several years. Sometimes the woman would return in her dreams, melancholic and alone, sitting on the edge on an upside-down small boat, crying and calling her soul pieces to return. However, Whalina had pushed the quest to fill the void of the woman's soul to the very back of her mind, until today.

"So, there. That's all there is to it." She gathered her things as the train approached its final stop.

"Thank you for sharing this with me, Ali. You'll get the answers you need; I'm sure of it." He wrapped his arms around her, waiting for the train door to open.

As they walked to her parents' restaurant, Whalina asked herself what exactly were the answers she was looking for. The thought that the painting was nothing but a childish fantasy gone wrong weighed heavily on her shoulders. What if, after all these years, she was opening a Pandora's box that was better left closed? The air was crisp, and her nose was rosy red from the cold as they entered the familiar family-run Mediterranean restaurant. Inside, everything seemed the same. The dark wooden tables were seaweed green, the chairs were still heavy, and the white walls were, as always, begging for colour, tired of their white-patterned wallpaper. In the middle of each table was a singular lit candle and around a full setup of impeccably polished wine glasses, plates, and silver cutlery. This had been Whalina's parents' first baby, then came Whalina, and finally, the surprise that no one had seen coming: Sarah.

"Whalina dear!" Her mother's high-pitched voice carried across the large restaurant. Teresa wore an elegant grey dress, thoughtfully matching the golden frame of the latest designer glasses on her face. Whalina was not surprised by her mother's cold hands as they embraced, for they were always cold—poor circulation, the doctor had told her.

"I've missed you, darling," she whispered, holding Whalina close.

"Missed you too, Mum." Whalina pulled away as soon as her dad emerged from the kitchen. Edward gave the warmest hugs in the world and somehow always managed to make Whalina feel as though she was still and always would be his little girl.

They sat at the table closest to the kitchen, the same one each time they ate at the restaurant. When Whalina and her sister were younger, they had spent countless hours at this table, as both their parents had been busy running the restaurant. Whalina eyed the empty chair which her younger sister would always occupy and felt a numbing emptiness.

"My golden girl," Teresa said, gently stroking Whalina's face.

"Mum, stop fussing please." She moved her head away.

"Can I not be happy to see my beautiful daughter? And to think we almost lost you in that horrible accident." Teresa finally withdrew her hand as a young waitress placed a range of meze dips and salads on the table.

Ever since she could remember, Whalina had always been the golden child, whereas they would treat Sarah as a mistimed accident. Whist her parents had been eager to expand the business and send Whalina to school, the morning sickness and, later, the late-night feeds had gotten in the way of opening a second branch. Only two months after the untimely daughter had been born, Teresa hired a nanny, and Sarah would never feel the warmth of her mother's breast again. The younger daughter had invisible bars she needed to reach through to access her mother's love—bars which Whalina had never experienced but, nevertheless, had involuntarily helped to set. Continuously compared with her oldest sister's grades, behaviour, and achievements no matter the depth of desire and effort, Sarah could never keep up. In the end, she had given in and stopped trying altogether. Despite being offered a prestigious place at Oxford University six months ago, Sarah had announced that she was going travelling with her boyfriend. Ignoring warnings of being cut out from the will and several arguments, the young adventure seeker had left for South America, paying the ultimate price of being denied any remaining love and approval from her mother.

"I ordered your favourite, Whalina, and the muhammara dip especially for you, Neal." Teresa looked genuinely pleased, and Whalina wondered whether her mother was truly incapable of reading the emotions of others or whether she simply did not care.

"When are you thinking of going back to work, sweetheart?" Edward asked between his bites of the Greek salad.

"I'm not sure, Dad. I think I need to take a break and think about where I'm heading." Whalina felt uneasy saying this in front of her parents, perhaps more so in front of her mother.

"You're not thinking of taking off and travelling the world, darling? This millennium trend of finding yourself hasn't gotten into you too, now, has it?" Teresa sounded as though she intended to be funny, like what she was saying was a joke or a rhetorical question not to be taken seriously.

"I hear Sarah landed safely in Ecuador." Whalina changed the subject, and her parents dropped their gazes to their plates. "She said Colombia was amazing. She and Mikey even spent some time in the jungle." She watched the stubborn pair fill their bodies with pride and ego. "They took part in this ceremony, and Sarah had—"

"We don't want to hear this, sweetheart," her mother said. "Your sister made her choices. Now please, has everyone finished? Shall I bring out the dessert, or should we take it to go?" The red lipstick lips sealed shut as the muscles around Teresa's jaw tightened. She placed the neatly folded linen napkin on the chair and stood. "I'll ask Dafni to pack a box to go." As soon as Teresa left the table, her thin lips curved into a customer-friendly smile, spreading across all corners of her face but the eyes.

"Dad, this is crazy. How long are you going to punish her for leaving?" Her cheeks pinkened when a young couple at the table across looked over.

"Honey, your mum just wants what's best for you and your sister." Edward's voice sounded strained, unmatching for his polite smile. That was one of the many things Whalina loved about her father: his gentle temper. Only, at times like this, it was a little too placid, and she wished he'd have the courage to stand up for what was right

"Mum thinks she knows what's best for everyone, but this whole family drama was created by her inability to let Sarah make her own choices." Whalina knew she had made a valid point, but before Edward and his grey beard had a chance to respond, Teresa had returned, holding a large bag filled with Turkish desserts.

The house was a short drive through the familiar backroads which would forever remain engraved in Whalina's memory. The neighbourhood was a part of her personal history. She had spent eighteen years living in the same house and bedroom, in which she collected the various souvenirs of a child and young adult. After she had packed the necessities into one small suitcase and left the family home for university, the room had remained the same, almost like she had never left. The old teddy bear won at a summer fair lay on the single bed, and next to it hung a list of school exam dates. Yet upon entering the house, Whalina felt foreign between the walls that had housed countless family memories and celebrations. That feeling was not unusual and had become so familiar that when it appeared, it quickly faded into the background, becoming the norm; not feeling at home was part of her identity.

Feeling like a visitor, Whalina removed her shoes at the door and nudged Neal to do the same. Apart from a new, thin burgundy carpet that went well with the cream sofa, everything else appeared unchanged.

"When was the last time you visited us, darling?" Teresa asked whilst unloading the desserts onto the dining table.

"I think it was a little before Sarah left." Whalina approached Teresa with four small plates from the kitchen, hoping her mother would not bring the lack of visits into the spotlight. The truth was that a part of her felt by visiting, she was betraying her little sister. By staying away, in her own way, Whalina could protest and subliminally say it had been wrong for her parents to shut out Sarah. Deep down, she was proud of her sister for taking an alternative route to life and wished for more courage to do the same.

"You know when Grandma Jenny died, I realised a few important home truths." Teresa paused, planting a face of sadness and remorse.

"Like what, Mum?" The evening was still young, and Whalina was already getting tired of Teresa's old tactics.

"That I should have visited her more often. I don't want the same for you, sweetie." Teresa's face grew in concern as she placed her hand over Whalina's forehead.

"You seem to be running a fever. Take off this woolly jumper, and here, take this."

Whalina took a pink pill from her mother's hand and swallowed it without thinking twice. She removed the thick jumper and, instead, covered her shoulders with a light cardigan Teresa had brought from upstairs. It smelled of the floral perfume Teresa would wear when Whalina was young. The smell triggered a memory she thought she had forgotten; the girls were full of energy, and it was Sarah's turn to hide and Whalina's turn to seek. Sarah had slipped on the wet floor and broken Teresa's wedding anniversary present: a rare, authentic ceramic vase worth thousands of pounds. Fortunately, Whalina had been the first to find her sister standing beside the broken vase, tongue twisted and motionless. Teresa had been next on the scene. Before Sarah could utter a word, Whalina had taken the blame, knowing the scolding would not be nearly as severe as the punishment Sarah would receive. The sense of responsibility was innate for Whalina, and there had been countless more incidents where she had used lies to protect her sister.

The floral perfume was the one Teresa had been wearing that day and served as a reminder that some things were best left unsaid in front of her mother. Whilst Teresa was brewing hot drinks in the kitchen, Whalina grew impatient, waiting for the right moment that might never arrive and, at last, took the opportunity to speak to Edward alone.

With his head down, the humble man left Neal to set up the Monopoly game alone and approached his daughter.

"What is it, my love? What's going on?" he whispered, scratching his head.

"Dad, I don't want you to worry, but …" Whalina held her breath and released a quiet sigh.

"Come on, now. You can tell your old man. What's troubling you, baby?" He placed his hand on her shoulder, reminding Whalina that Edward was not one to judge.

"Do you remember those paintings you took from my room when Mum and I went to Wales? I was about sixteen at the time." As though a heavy weight had been lifted, her shoulders dropped away from her ears.

Edward nodded, outing himself before he could contemplate on the right thing to say. Till this day, the mystery of this very painting had remained not only for its artist, but also her dad. Several blank canvases would be signed for at the door with his signature, only to be covered with the exact same image as its predecessor.

"Yes, I remember. You're not a child anymore; I suppose you would like them back?" he said quietly, looking deeply into Whalina's eyes, as if to say, *I hope you know what you are doing*.

Without waiting for an answer, together they walked through the warm drizzle to the end of the garden. The sun was minutes from setting, but enough light remained for Whalina to notice the small picture frame attached to Edward's bundle of keys, revealing the day of his sixtieth birthday as he stood between his daughters, who had their arms tightly wrapped around him. The garden shed's creaking door finally opened, and an old smell of wood welcomed them inside. The light switch was not working, but traces of the mellow sunset was enough to illuminate the weightless dust. Rusty gardening tools, cardboard boxes damaged with small mice holes, and ceramic flowerpots cluttered the space. At the end of the narrow shed, laying on a high shelf, were the abandoned canvases.

Recovering the part of Whalina's childhood that had been pushed aside, Edward pulled off the dusty cover. For over a decade, all eighteen pieces of the unfinished artwork had waited for a moment of praise and admiration.

Stepping on a small, two-step ladder, Whalina took one of the paintings into her hands.

"I'll leave you to it, sweetheart."

She turned and saw the door left wide open and her father no longer with her. She slowly descended the ladder and took down a handful of paintings, then lined the artwork against the wooden wall. She scanned each painting with a torch. Yet even today, she could not find a justification for the emphasis that she had placed on the colour of this woman's soul. The defeat she had felt as a child crept up on Whalina as she stood opposite the misunderstood alien fragments of her past.

"They all look the same …"

Whalina's shriek disturbed the enclosing silence.

"Sorry, I didn't mean to scare you. Think you could finish the painting now?" Neal wondered.

Without needing a moment to think, she answered, "Not then, and not now. Maybe never." Through a long, deep sigh, she realised she had accepted the void both in the canvas and in herself. "Oddly enough, I can resonate with her." Whalina's posture mirrored the figure's stance, and with her arms and ankles crossed, she confessed, "The woman in the painting—, I can see myself in her."

She sauntered towards the third painting of the displayed art. This was the only one which still had a perfectly white and empty space. It had not aged, and no dust coloured it grey. The blank canvas held a certain type of promise for redemption, as though it could still be saved. Whalina squatted until her eyes were level with the woman's eyes of power and strength in the painting. She stowed the other paintings on the shelf and placed the painting with the clean, vacant soul space under her arm. She sealed the crumbling door, and with Neal leading the way through the moonlit sky, they returned to the house. Whalina's heart was beating faster than usual, making itself known to her.

As she entered the house, her head spun, narrowing her vision and making it impossible to stand. Her legs turned to jelly, as though something was sucking the living energy from her being, forcing her to sit.

"Al, what's going on?" Neal stood in front of her, not releasing her bare shoulders.

"Water, I need water," Whalina whispered, and Edward was already there, handing her a glass. She gulped down a whole glass in one go and asked for a second one, which she proceeded to finish as quickly as she did the first one.

"Sweetheart, is it the painting? Are you sure this is a good idea?"

Whalina looked into her father's frightened eyes; she hated being the cause of his worry.

"I'm absolutely fine, just felt a little lightheaded, that's all." She got up as if to prove nothing worthy of concern was happening to her.

"What painting, Edward?"

Whalina sighed deeply from hearing her mother's voice from the kitchen.

"It's nothing, Mum! Just an old painting I think it's time to finish," she shouted back, reassuring her mother, and hurriedly hid the canvas inside her bag in vain, for she was too late.

"Why are you taking this?" Teresa stood tall with her hands mounted on her hips.

"Because it's mine, Mum. What are you going to do about it? Stop talking to me like you did with Sarah?" Whalina was as surprised at herself as everyone else in the room.

"It's for your own good. Give it here!" Teresa reached out expectantly.

Whalina stood motionless as she hesitated to do what she knew was right. "No. I'm not a child anymore, and I, just like Sarah, make my own choices." Her voice was soft, but behind it was enormous power as she uncovered her strength.

"What are you trying to prove? That, just like your sister, you know what's best for you? She is throwing her life away with that boy and doing God knows what instead of building her future," Teresa shouted behind her as she walked towards the front door.

"Sarah did something no one in this family had the guts to do. Instead of being proud of your courageous daughter, you shut her out, because she didn't do as she was told." Whalina put on her shoes as fast as possible, eager to flee.

"If you just picked up the phone and called her, you'd know how wrong you are," she said, knowing it was the right thing to say and to stand up for her sister. For the past six months, Whalina had felt like a bystander watching her mother push her little sister aside once again.

"My relationship with Sarah is my own. All I have ever wanted was keep you girls safe, and I know this painting is nothing but trouble. Now please come back inside." Teresa was forced to calm down as Whalina stood with one foot out the door where the heavy rain was forming small rivers on the street.

"Maybe so, Mum, but it's my trouble." Whalina knew the painting represented a piece of her shadow self. Despite the foreboding feeling that her mother was right, she felt compelled to do what she had started.

"Alright, have it your way, just please don't leave the house the way your sister did." Teresa appeared ten years older as her sad eyes clung onto the last fading piece of hope.

Whalina could not bring herself to shut the door on her parents and leave without saying something she had been waiting to say all evening. "Call her, please. She is hurting just as much as you are."

Teresa nodded neither in agreement nor argument.

Whalina opened her arms and hugged her mother close, knowing that behind the steel façade, her mother did want what was best for her children; perhaps her heart's intentions were somewhat merged with her know-it-all ego, but deep down, she really did care.

"Get home safe now, and watch this fever, darling." Teresa planted a final kiss on Whalina's forehead.

The hard rain turned into a light drizzle, and Edward offered to drive them to the train station. Whist they waited for the traffic lights to turn green, a feeling of déjà vu rose inside Whalina. Of course, she had been at this junction many times before; it was familiar yet oddly different. Neal was sitting in the back seat instead of Sarah, and she was no longer a child but a woman with a world and life of her own. There was no sign of the two ponytails tied back with pink headbands but, instead, the simple yet elegant arrangement of her long hair to its side.

Whalina noticed her father was looking down at the canvas.

"Dad, it's green."

She took him out of the deep valley of thoughts, and he rapidly pressed his foot to accelerate. Whalina silently hoped that before they reached the station, he would say what was on his mind, but the roads were empty, and they ran out of time.

"Thank you for the ride, Dad. It was really good to see you."

They embraced and held each other longer than usual.

"I've missed you, darling. I'm very proud of you and the woman you've become," he whispered whilst still holding her close.

"Thank you, Dad …" She paused, knowing something else needed to be said.

"Don't worry about the painting; I can handle it. And one more thing. Sarah misses you, and we both love you so much," she assured him and placed a big kiss on the lightly wrinkled cheek.

The clock was approaching eleven at night, and the last train was waiting for departure. Seconds before the door closed, they jumped onto the empty train and waved through the window to Edward, who stood faithfully on the platform. The train moved forward, and Whalina's reflection appeared on the dirty glass. Small grey bags underlined her eyes, and she looked how she felt: worn out.

With open arms, Neal took the window seat and invited Whalina to rest her head on his comfortable warm chest. The train quietly rocked, and Whalina felt safe as a baby in its mother's arms.

"I know how much that painting means to you. I'm glad you got it back," Neal whispered close to her ear and softly caressed her knuckles. No words were needed, the silence allowed for mutual understanding and the enjoyment of the simplicity of a quiet train ride.

Whalina closed her eyes for what she thought was a moment. When she opened them again, unexpected movement between the two front seats stole her attention. Through the small gap between the chairs, she saw an open book held by feeble, feminine hands. Being a reader herself and curious to see what story lay between the pages, she squinted her hazel eyes to sharpen the vision, and the words magnified: *If you are yearning to come home, look out for the signs around you. Listen to the voice inside, and the way home will be revealed to you.* The book abruptly closed, leaving Whalina eager to read more.

Gently freeing herself from Neal's heavy arms, she stood over the owner of the book. "Would you mind sharing the title of your book with me?"

With eyes big as an owl's and blue like the cloudless sky, an older woman looked up in response. "Would you like a seat, dear?" She proffered her hand, and Whalina touched the ice-cold wrinkly hand in front of her. An instant wave of goosebumps travelled down her body like the strongest of all ocean currents.

Feeling obliged to accept the invitation, she took the seat next to the elderly lady with long, wavy grey hair and a beautiful white flower behind her right ear.

"And what is your name?" Her voice was feeble and thin, fragile like glass that might break at any moment.

"Whalina. My name is Whalina, and your name?" She tried hard to look into the woman's eyes just like mother had taught her. Whalina could not break away from the mesmerising leaf-shaped golden buttons clasped all the way up on the impeccably white coat.

"Sacnicte. Is there something you would like to ask?"

Bewildered by how peculiar the old woman was, a hundred questions rushed through Whalina's mind. "I didn't mean to pry. I accidentally saw the book you were reading and was wondering what it's about?" She met Sacnicte's eyes.

After a moment, the old woman responded, "Why is my book important to you?"

Risking sounding as weird as the woman next to her, Whalina admitted, "Because it spoke of going home." She contemplated what might be the right thing to say next but found a higher power was in charge of her voice. "Sacnicte, do you think there is a home out there, somewhere, where I belong?" Heat rushed across her face.

"Why, of course, child." Sacnicte had no problem with eye contact and fixated on Whalina's. "When you reach that place, you will know in your heart and soul that you're home. Tell me, are you happy here?"

Speaking even softer than before, Whalina concentrated on each word. "Yes, I'm happy … somewhat happy." She could lie to herself but not to Sacnicte; the mature woman deserved the truth.

"What are you missing?" The blue eyes briefly shone brightly.

"A purpose." Put on the spot, Whalina heard her voice breaking.

"It is your duty to find a way home, child. Don't wait. Do it before you get old like I have. Live before you die." Sacnicte took the flower from her hair and neatly tucked it behind Whalina's ear. "It's my station. I'm getting off the train. It's time that you do too. Don't miss your stop, dear."

And in a blink of an eye, Sacnicte was gone.

CHAPTER 8

WALKING ON WATER

Time: The Last Night
Location: The Fallen Kingdom of Light

The sun had finally set, and the full moon had taken its place. The hot day was turning into a cool night, and the howling winds rushed through the forest trees, scattering leaves in fury. Remedy regretted her decision to walk barefoot. Although it made her feel calmer and more grounded, the lack of light made it difficult to see what lay on the path ahead. The burning in the arch of her left foot was indicative of a cut, and she was determined to ensure it would be the first and last injury of the night. Without a map, she had no choice but to rely on her intuition to get home. The landscape looked very different in the dark, and she struggled to differentiate between the forest trees. The idea of going home to see her parents, who seemed oblivious as to why she could possibly be so moved by her grandmother's death, made her nearly as furious as the branch-breaking wind.

Sacnicte had taught her how to understand the woods. Remedy could feel their sadness and despair. It was only her parents who had seemed so passive and immaculately collected at the funeral, but, of course, everyone was once they discovered their purpose. It was as though knowing why they were born gave people internal peace to such a degree that they believed no matter what happened, everything was and would be well. Remedy thought it was foolishly naive to be so detached from the reality and to accept everything for what it was.

Although her parents were not completely indifferent to Sacnicte's death, as Papa did seem a little uneasy, it certainly did not cause such an emotional upheaval as it did in Remedy. Walking towards the moonlight, she wondered whether she too would be as placid and even-tempered as her parents once she learned her purpose. What would life be like once her emotions regulated to an all-time state of contentment and peace? Would it truly be liberating for her eyes to only see the good in every person and to accept every situation for what it was? For the first time, she even wondered what life would be like if she had never found out her purpose and, instead, lived an idle life and died without leaving her mark on the world. *Could it be possible to live without a purpose and still be happy?*

Before her heart had a chance to answer, her mind quickly pushed aside the thought, remembering that her grandmother had dedicated her life to helping people discover their purpose, and that still meant something to Remedy. Sacnicte couldn't possibly have been wrong about it all. Regardless whether her personality would change once she learned her purpose, Remedy couldn't let go of the idea that it must be rewarding in so many ways, for life to have meaning and to live for more than personal pleasures.

The path ahead forked, and Remedy had to choose between the smooth, sandy trail and the uneven ground filled with stones and twigs. The sandy trail appeared easier on the feet, but the tall trees blocked any remaining moonlight; on the other hand, the rocky road seemed brighter yet most definitely harder to traverse. The soft sand was a relief for Remedy's beaten-up feet as she cautiously stepped onto the darker path. Apart from the occasional rustling of leaves, the wind seemed to have calmed down, and an eerie silence filled the woods. Remedy made no sound as she glided through the sand and, after a while, wondered whether she had, in fact, taken the right path.

A sudden noise, like a large object or branch had fallen into a pile of leaves, surprised her, and all wondering ceased. Remedy stood still, listening anxiously, yet all she heard was her fast-beating heart hitting against her fragile chest. She knew the night itself could not harm her, yet her human instincts advised otherwise.

"Remedy," the darkness said, heavy and ever so low, making her name sound like a song.

Remedy stood still, holding her breath.

"Remedy," the voice sang.

Although Remedy could not see anything, she looked from side to side, desperately hoping to find a shape or a colour—anything to tell her what she was up against. An ash-like smell rose in the air, irritating and clogging the inside of her throat.

"I've been waiting for you, Remedy." The husky voice was closer, louder, and deeper, as though darkness had been smoking a thick cigar, and the smoke had not yet left his lungs.

Remedy stood paralyzed, unable to answer or move her feet as they sunk deeper into what no longer had the consistency of sand but rather a thick, warm liquid. For the first time in her life, she experienced real-time fear, an immediate threat, and in that moment, she was certain something had changed in the Kingdom of Light.

"What do you want?" Remedy recovered her voice and found courage knowing she had been born a guardian of the land, and it was her duty to protect it. The deafening silence changed tone, and a high-pitched sound rang through Remedy's head. It felt as though a decade of persistent hissing had passed, when suddenly foreign hands pushed her to the ground.

"Get off me!" She kicked and punched the empty air.

"Remedy, calm down. It's me, Kai!"

"Kai? What are you doing here?"

"I could ask you the same thing." He pulled Remedy to her feet.

She hesitated to answer, unsure whether her mind was playing tricks on her or whether something or someone was lurking in the shadows of darkness.

"I'm a little lost. Can you point me towards the palace?" She peered into the darkness and allowed the foreign yet somehow known hands lead her towards the light.

Remedy had met Kai in the forest of Adamah when she was a young girl. The two used to play and explore the forest together until they had both become old enough to recognise their differences. Remedy and her family were all about traditions, whereas Kai didn't believe in destiny and the idea of living for purpose. It was just him and his father, hidden away in the darkest spot of the forest, where they liked to keep to themselves.

Kai took Remedy's hand and guided her to where she had come from. His eyes seemed to have adjusted to the darkness, and he quickly

navigated to the rocky path towards the moonlight. The moon illuminated Kai's kind golden eyes, and Remedy felt safe once she saw his
face. His teeth were pearl white, and he smiled from the eyes, making
her feel easy in his presence. His long, bouncy curls blew with the
warm wind, and Remedy ran her hands through her own tangled hair.

"Your feet don't look so good," Kai said, and they both looked at
the bleeding cuts.

"They will heal by the morning," she said nonchalantly, as though
the cuts had not been stinging. She wanted to look brave in front of
him.

"I'll carry you until the ground evens." Before Remedy could object, Kai's strong arms had wrapped securely over her small body, and
he walked effortlessly on the rocky ground.

Being cradled with great care made her feel safe and secure, as
though she was a child. She buried her head into his naked chest and
closed her eyes, smelling a scent of sweet floral jasmine on his skin. It
had a subtle yet rich woody musk, which reminded her of the dazzling
jasmine trees by his small wooden house, the place where, once upon
a time, she visited nearly every day. The smell brought back memories
of the adventures they used to have, chasing butterflies and spending
their summers swimming in the nearby river. Life seemed simple back
when they had lived an innocent existence with no labels, family his-
tories, and expectations.

"Kai, can I ask you something?" Remedy said softly.

"What is it, Sunny?" Kai said with a hint of nostalgia.

Remedy's heart skipped a beat, remembering the first time Kai
had called her that name. When they had been about eight years old,
they spent their afternoons watching the sunset whilst eating sunflower seeds. One day, Remedy had visited his house, carrying a
massive sunflower, with its roots intact and all. Wanting to surprise
him, she had ripped the flower with full force from Sacnicte's garden
and sprinted to Kai's house. From that day onwards, Kai had called her
Sunny girl.

"The ground is soft. You can walk here."

Remedy reluctantly stepped on the moist soil, and they walked in
silence towards the moonlight.

"So, what did you want to ask me?"

Remedy sighed, and instead of asking Kai the question she had first intended, she looked at her feet and said, "My grandmother died this morning."

Kai murmured something, then said, "I am sorry to hear that." He sounded genuine, but Remedy could tell something was holding him back.

At last, bright lights appeared ahead, bringing to light the unbearable tension between them. Whalina felt the words that had been left unspoken rising through the silent space. "Is that all you have to say?" Her voice sounded angrier than she had wanted.

"We're from two different worlds, Remedy. I cannot change who I am," he said, confirming what, deep down, Remedy already knew. Kai was not a guardian of the land; he came from an ordinary family of wood-makers who didn't believe in such a thing as destiny.

Kai's mother had left his dad right after Kai was born, with the pretence that it was her life purpose calling her. Ever since Kai had learnt the truth, he decided no matter what his life purpose was, he would always create his own destiny. Several months ago, she and Kai had argued and couldn't agree on their two very different viewpoints. Remedy was convinced that Kai would hinder her ability to protect and guide the people of the land if he did not believe in her cause. With the belief that she was acting in line with her duty as a guardian, she had pulled away from Kai, losing one of the few people who truly understood her. Their two stubborn heads couldn't find their way back to each other until today.

Finally, they reached the end of the path, and the ocean was clear on the horizon. They stood at the top of the green hill and gazed into the empty space above the kingdom. Remedy now knew where she was but would not leave without confirming she would see Kai again.

"I'm sorry for everything, Kai. I never meant to make you feel like you were not good enough."

"You know the way back home from here," he said with a small, forced smile.

"Can you walk with me? Of course, if you're not needed somewhere else ..." she responded, allowing herself to be vulnerable to rejection.

"I can walk with you."

She smiled inside, and they descended the hill towards the ocean, and somehow, Remedy's hand found his. Kai's hands were much stronger and larger than she remembered as a kid. They were rough from all the woodworking Kai did with his father, and Remedy felt nostalgic remembering the wooden figures they used to carve. He was wearing the wooden watch she had carved for his fifteenth birthday. Perhaps he was also missing her as much as she did him.

By the time they reached sea level, most lights were out, and the kingdom was asleep. The sky was perfectly black, and whilst walking in the empty streets, Remedy felt the vastness of space. She was but a speck of dust in the grand scheme of the universe, and for a moment, she thought of herself foolish for ever believing that her small, insignificant self could ever make a difference to the world.

"Do you think that one person can change the world?" she asked, confident that Kai would understand her question in a way no one else could.

"Even the smallest stone once thrown on water can cause the largest ripples, so yes, I think you can change the world, Remedy." And there it was, the look in his eyes again which softened her heart every time and again.

Remedy felt déjà vu as they were about to turn their backs to the ocean and walk towards the palace. Despite the wind that night, the water appeared still in the distance, and Remedy remembered seeing it the same way that morning when she had decided to fly to the garden to meet her grandmother. She had wanted to turn back then but didn't.

"I need to check something." She pulled Kai towards the ocean, her little feet walking double her usual speed, then triple as she neared the shore. "The water … how is this possible?" she panted.

Kai released her hand, knelt, and ran his hand over the smooth surface. "Hard as a rock." He stepped his right foot on the suspended-in-time ocean.

"Don't—" Remedy stammered, wanting to approach this in the only way she knew how.

"Come closer, Sunny." He extended his hand towards her.

Remedy slowly retreated.

Papa must see this. Something is wrong." Her head spun as her heart beat in double time.

"There's no use doing that, Sunny. He will tell you it's for the greater good," he teased.

Deep down, Remedy knew Kai was right. Her parents wouldn't even consider investigating her grandmother's death. No questions, no discussion, they accepted everything for what it was. But this, right here, she needed to do this without them.

Kai's kind smile encouraged her, and she reached for him, stepping carefully on the cool, hard surface. It wasn't frozen cold, as she expected, but simply frozen in time, leaving Remedy speechless. They walked silently on the water, expecting cracks on the unknown surface which, to their surprise, remained perfectly intact. Even in the land where nothing was impossible, this was unlike anything Remedy had ever seen before.

Walking deeper across the ocean, she felt a black hole drilling into the pit of her stomach, the feeling of fear manifesting inside. The air pressure was heavy, turning breathing into an oppressive discomfort. "What's happening?"

"Looks like we are frozen in time," Kai answered quietly.

"But, Kai, the moon controls the oceans, and the moon works together with the sun. Some things can never change." She looked up and waited for him to notice her.

Kai spoke without flinching or changing his forward-facing gaze. "There are forces at play other than destiny, Remedy."

Although she could not see the storm ahead, the strong smell indicated that it was close, and Remedy knew in her gut that life would never be the same. She eyed Kai again, and this time, he met her gaze. He had kind eyes, ones she was certain she could trust. Kai gently tilted her chin towards him and looked deeply into her eyes. Remedy felt his gaze penetrate through and see her naked soul, and it allowed her to experience the warm light of his soul. She was sorry for the time they had lost together but knew those times were over now. Seeing him through the eyes of his soul, she could sense the immense power within him and was sure he would always be a part of her destiny.

Kai pulled her close and kissed her deeply. It was long enough for her to inhale his breath and feel the warmth of his skin. The moment felt eternal, and nothing else existed in their universe. Remedy's feet weakened as his arms pulled her closer, their bodies intertwining like the most perfect labyrinth. Her gut forgot the fear she had felt just moments ago, and, instead, hundreds of butterflies were let free, forward flipping in her stomach a thousand times and making her feel as though she could fly. Her heart beat in a way it had never done before; she felt alive.

CHAPTER 9

GOLDEN MOMENTS

After coming home from her parents' house and having the painting back in her hands, Whalina felt different. Laying in bed that night felt different. The last time Whalina remembered feeling this way was graduation, the night when she and Neal had crossed the friendship boundary, and they entered a romantic relationship.

The pillow appeared softer, more soothing to the mind that was already dreaming. In dreamland, Whalina swam through a jungle of tall trees and high grass, navigating blindly yet fiercely as ever and determined to get to the finish line in time. Time was of the essence, and the race was not for herself but for a larger collective that depended on her reaching the end point in time. The grass cut through her naked body, and she prayed to see the sun again. Someone must have heard her prayer, as the dark shadows above dissolved, and the sun penetrated through, allowing her sunken eyes to see that she had arrived.

With blood upon her face and hands black from mud, she emerged from the ground with a burning sensation spreading from her chest. Before she could see the colour of the flaming fire inside, a noise from another world brought her back. Whalina scrambled for the phone that had dropped to the floor. "Hello?" Whalina's voice was rusty.

"Oh God. I woke you up. Sorry, sorry, go back to sleep," Sarah frantically apologised.

"No, it's okay. Are you all right? Did something happen?" Whalina sat upright in bed.

"Nothing happened. I just really miss you." Hearing her baby sister desperately trying to stifle her tears broke Whalina's heart.

"Honey, you can always come home. We're here waiting for you." Her own eyes welled.

"You're my home, Ali. I'm happy here, but you're missing. I wish I could just get one of your big sister hugs; it's been too long."

Whalina's sense of obligation and responsibility for Sarah was being poked in a familiar way. Hearing the soft voice break and being distanced with over five thousand miles weighed heavily on Whalina. From the moment of holding her new-born sister, she had taken the role of the big sister quite seriously. Being witness to each phrase of Sarah's life, she oddly felt like her second mother. "Sarah sweetie, wipe your tears. Where are you right now?"

"Ecuador."

Suddenly, Whalina knew exactly where she was heading.

*****

After she had thought about it all day, the news was bursting to escape and be shared. The plane tickets were reasonably priced; South America was a foreign continent promising grand adventures, and most importantly, Sarah was there. Whalina paused the film but continued to watch the frozen screen as though nothing had changed.

"Why did you pause it?" Neal asked, reaching for the bowl of popcorn and eyeing Whalina.

"What do you think of Ecuador?" she asked to test the waters.

"I read that it's one of the most biodiverse places in the world, and it's on the equator. That's pretty much all I … And, of course, your sister is there."

Without needing to test any more waters, Whalina stepped fully into the pool and heard her heart speak without barriers. "It would only be for a few weeks, and God knows we both need a break and to step off this crazy train. Please come with me." Whalina regarded Neal with bright eyes full of hope. She told herself not to get too excited, but her emotions were difficult to contain.

"Please, please, *please* …" She elongated the last letters for as long as her breath allowed.

Neal had to think about the logistics for a day, but deep down, they knew they'd follow each other to the end of the world. A week later, they flew to Quito, the capital of Ecuador, via alongside the longest continental mountain range in the world; the Andean Mountains were endless to the human eye from above. The grand mountains had unique wrinkles, creases, and sharp peaks; no picture could tell their story better than they could themselves. The grand collision of the South American and Pacific tectonic plates over fifty million years ago could not fit into a singular picture frame. The endless peaks were home to both dormant and active volcanoes, some too small for human eyes to see in the boundless space beneath the plane.

Looking down, Whalina witnessed the physical distance they had crossed, yet it oddly felt like the destination would be home. Leaving England and handing in her resignation letter at work was like saying goodbye to a boarding school. It was now that real life would start and the journey back home to herself would truly begin. She promised herself that when she returned, she would first complete her painting, then fulfil her long-time dream to open an art gallery.

Walking out from Arrivals, Whalina scanned the crowd and spotted Sarah, the only European standing amid the Latin American crowd. The blond-bleached hair had been cut, and in its place was the mousey brown that Sarah had been born with, long enough to gently brush the shoulders. The meeting of their eyes instigated an instant rush of adrenaline to their legs to push through the crowd, and they met in a deep embrace. The much-missed smell of vanilla filled Whalina's senses, her sister's signature smell. She could recognise it anywhere. The whole world ceased to exist, their brains paused, and all that mattered was they were together again.

"Was this the hug you were after?" Whalina whispered, holding Sarah close.

"Yes, but I'm not letting you go just yet." Sarah squeezed Whalina as much as she could, and the sisters broke out in a carefree laughter infused with tears.

"I cannot believe you actually came." With a tight grip around Whalina's arms and eyes filled with awe, Sarah regarded her sister with slight disbelief, checking that she was really here, in the flesh.

"It's not every day that your baby sis wakes you up, crying in the middle of the night. Come here," she said with a sigh of relief and co-

cooned Sarah inside her arms. Witnessing her safe and sound in the flesh was an entirely different experience than the video calls and texts they had shared over the past months. Even though it was the longest time they had gone without seeing each other, it felt like only yesterday when they were drinking coffee in one of London's fancy cafés and discussing Sarah's new adventure.

"And where's my hug?" Neal asked lightheartedly, and Sarah leapt from her sister's arms into his.

After collecting their luggage, they took a taxi to the hostel which would be their home for the next couple days. The flight back to England was in three weeks, and Whalina had carefully planned the trip, making each day count. Allowing a few days to become acclimated to the high altitude, they would stay in the city and explore the surrounding towns and various markets. Whalina and Neal would then travel south to Baños and go hiking, whilst Sarah returned to volunteering in the indigenous community, where her boyfriend, Mikey, was waiting for her. Together they were helping the shamans with the propagation of medicinal plants, as well as taking part and assisting in shamanic ceremonies and teachings for truth seekers coming from all over the world. This was where Whalina and Neal planned to go after the hike before returning to England.

The modest yet comfortable hostel was located in the old town, and straight after checking in, Sarah took her guests on a small tour. Founded in the sixteenth century, the old town was South America's least-altered historic centre. Not only were the manmade wonders well preserved, contributing to the feeling of being in a foreign world—perhaps even a film set in a different era—but nature had also played its part. The ancient fathers, the mountains around Quito, stood tall and were visible from any part of the city, adding to the surreal atmosphere. Mountains in every direction enclosed the city, whilst inside, dazzling neo-Gothic churches and monasteries filled the town plaza.

Surrounded by the Spanish tongue and small streets, Whalina noticed a smell that was hard to ignore permeate the air. It was not a bad smell, and although it could not be named or described, it fostered a feeling of safety and freedom that only Whalina could sense. "What is this smell?"

"The smell of fish? I know you wouldn't expect that in a place nearly three-thousand metres above sea level." Sarah pointed to the Basilica of the National Vow, the oldest church in Ecuador. It looked back with an omniscient presence as it towered overlooking the capital.

"It's not fish. The closest thing it resembles is a feeling of something good coming." Whalina realised the words made no sense as soon as she said them.

"Feelings don't have smells, Whally. I think you're hungry for some yuca." Sarah continued speaking in a Spanish accent, embodying the role of a tour guide. She shared her newly acquired knowledge of the native South American dishes, explaining that yuca is a root vegetable with the texture of a potato and tastes somewhat nutty and sweet.

Moments later, they were seated in an Ecuadorian café, anticipating the promised yuca. The trio also enjoyed freshly fried plantain, empanadas, and humitas. Whalina attempted to converse with the waiter, using whatever could be remembered from the years of Spanish classes at school, which, after all, did not amount to much. They spent the rest of the day roaming aimlessly around shops and market stands, browsing through traditional Ecuadorian products, such as ponchos, hats, woollen blankets, as well as chocolate and coffee. Exhausted from their travel across the Atlantic Ocean and Sarah's brilliant but tiring tour, they finally returned to the hostel.

Whalina felt a migraine coming on, and instead of listening to her body's pleas for rest, she swallowed a painkiller. Whilst Neal read a book in bed, the sisters explored the hostel's small but charming garden, which would soon be witness to their late-night heart-to-heart talk. The Ecuadorian sky lacked the light pollution found so easily across London, which allowed the dark sky its privacy, unseen by others. Whatever the sky was occupied with during its sleepless nights would be protected from the judgements of the average human being. Only the awakened ones could understand the stories of love and loss told by the empty sky.

Glass lanterns, hanging from the trees, lit the path towards the back of the garden and illuminated the lone bench. The sisters sat, and Sarah's head rested on Whalina's lap when they mentioned the subject of their parents.

"Have you spoken to Mum and Dad today?" She turned her head to face Whalina.

"No. They don't even know I'm here."

Whalina was not surprised when Sarah sat upright and looked wide eyed at her. "But why? Did something happen?"

Whalina sighed deeply before recounting the recent dinner with her parents, missing no detail but of the painting. "Mum pretended you don't exist, and my resentment towards her grew." The words spread a deep, motionless silence across the garden, where only the crickets were audible. Even though contact between Teresa and Sarah had been severed for months, Whalina could see that her sister was not bitter nor sad; what she saw was hope.

"Mum loves you a lot, Whally, and she loves me as much as she can."

Overwhelmed by Sarah's words, Whalina felt her eyes water. She had never been prouder of her little sister. It was not the first time that she had thought, if only possible, she would gladly relinquish her mother's love if it meant that for once, Sarah did not have to decide between the love of her parents and her own happiness. Somehow, the world always asked her to decide, and Whalina was deeply touched that her sister had found a way to exhibit nothing but compassion and understanding for their mother.

"When did you become so wise?" Whalina lightly wiped the tear that had escaped her eye, and for a change, it was Sarah who placed her arms around her big sister's shoulders.

Something extraordinary happens when an individual leaves the safety net of a familiar environment and ventures into the den of the unknown. New roots emerge, and the flower flourishes in a way it never has before. What the flower believed in prior to leaving the familiar land is replaced with wisdom created through personal experience that could be gained nowhere else but in the field of the unknown. The unknown will expose the flower to new cultures, ways of living, problems, and challenges that nothing but life itself can prepare the flower for. It will rain and pour down, pushing the flower to its limits, and when the flower begins to drown, something magical will happen. The flower will not only survive, it will begin to thrive; this is exactly what happened to Sarah. Leaving a small town and venturing into the unknown lands of South America, Sarah had no idea how much her life would change. An unstoppable growth monster had been un-leashed, and this very monster had become her saviour.

"A lot has happened in the last six months," Sarah said, elusive as ever, yet it was enough for Whalina to understand the Sarah she knew before was gone. "I guess it all kicked off in the Sacred Valley in Peru. That's the first time we met Wind, our shaman." Sarah paused as though she could hear her sister's mind.

"Shaman? Is it like an exorcist or something?"

The girls laughed simultaneously, recreating the adult version of a sleepover. Instead of hot cocoa and magazines, they shared a bottle of Argentinian red wine, whilst Sarah shared the teachings that plant medicine had taught her. Shamans are the bridge between the human and spirit world. They lead ancient spiritual practices of the indigen-ous cultures, and it was a shaman who had introduced and prepared Sarah for her ayahuasca journey. Ayahuasca is a blend of two plants that the indigenous people of the Amazon had first formulated. Once the Banisteriopsis caapi and a shrub called Psychotria viridisare com-bine, they become ready for consumption, creating various psyche-delic, out-of-this-world effects. For Sarah, the plant medicine had been extremely healing.

"Whally, I tell you, one night with ayahuasca is like the ten years you've had with Pedro."

The girls laughed at the idea of Pedro taking part in a ceremony to get rid of all the baggage that he took on and absorbed from his pa-tients over the years.

"What's the biggest take away you've learnt?" Whalina asked, wondering if perhaps there was something that would help resolve her own internal turmoil, which she spared her sister from hearing.

"It's not something that is learnt; it's more of an internal experi-ence, a feeling, an understanding at a cellular level." Sarah shared the most beautiful lesson that Mother Ayahuasca had engraved in her heart: the lesson of self-love. The idea of self-love, the realisation that love is the most healing of all, is the same love each heart carries but is the most difficult to access. The unconditional acceptance and in-ternal feeling of belonging regardless of all other external factors, that is the power of self-love. Sarah's wound would only get deeper and more infected as the search for love took place outside herself. Abandoning Teresa's ideas and leaving the country, knowing her mother wanted nothing to do with her, broke Sarah's heart, and the flaming anger turned it into stone. During one of the ceremonies, Mother Ayahuasca had drawn a picture of a heart split into five chambers. Each fragmented part represented a source of love: parental, romantic, friendship, community, and in the top left corner was self-love. The images played like an animation, bringing attention to the illustrated lock around the self-love chamber, which could only be opened once that chamber was full. Ayahuasca showed Sarah that to heal the other segments of her heart, the most valuable box needed to be full first, and only when that happens could love overflow to the neighbouring chambers. The spiritual experience allowed Sarah to not only forgive her mother but to feel empathy and love for her.

"Mum is on her own journey, a journey we know nothing about, and what she has done to me is not wrong; it's not right, it just is."

The tables had turned; for the first time, Whalina felt equal to Sarah, knowing her little sister was more than capable of taking care of herself. Stunned by the non-judgmental standpoint and wisdom witnessed for the first time, she asked, "Do you think I could maybe do this ayahuasca thing sometime?"

Sarah's eyed beamed with light and enthusiasm. "I was hoping you'd ask," she replied with a smile that would shine through to the following morning.

The sisters finished their bottle of wine, drawing the night to an end. With no peculiar dreams, Whalina slept better than ever before and awoke to the feeling of someone lovingly rubbing her back.

"Time to wake up, sleepyhead. We have plenty to do today."

Whalina turned around and laughed as soon as her eyes opened.

Sarah was frozen in her famous funny face, her green eyes fixated on the bottom of her nose, tongue out and twisted to the left. It was the face of a child escaping realism. Sarah had learnt to pull that face as soon as she had developed the idea of the self, understanding that life can be lived from the inside of one's imagination. Whenever someone would say something that she had no desire to hear, the face would appear, and Sarah would play dead.

The memory ignited a warm, fuzzy feeling inside Whalina's chest, reminding her of the good times they had shared, the times where innocence and grand hopes for the future had lived.

"It's so bright outside. What time is it?" She scanned the room for Neal.

"He's in the shower. Time for you to get up. Chop-chop!" Sarah clapped her hands and gave Whalina ten minutes to get ready whilst she ordered breakfast.

They swiftly put into action the plan for the next few hours, and they spent the first part of the day at the TelefériQo—a gondola lift running from the edge of the city centre, all the way up to the east side of the Pichincha Volcano.

"How do we know it won't erupt?" Whalina asked, sitting in the aerial lift which would rise over two thousand linear metres.

"I suppose we don't. Hey, tour guide, when did this thing last erupt?" Neal turned to Sarah, who was recording a video of their ascent, featuring mainly lonely cows scattered on the fields below the gondola—fields greener than any countryside field Whalina had seen before.

Sarah turned the camera to face the lift's passengers. "The last eruption was in two thousand and two. How does that make you feel?"

"Terrified," Whalina said in a serious tone.

Neal immediately followed with, "I believe our fate has been sealed."

Light laughter, conceived by the futile hope of youth, filled the sky tram. Sarah immortalised the moment through the means of the camera, and although they did not know it then, the content of the clip would be replayed throughout the many years to come, not because of the Ecuadorian cows in the background—although beautiful, they would be briefly noticed. The video clip encapsulated the last golden memory. It was the beginning of the end.

PART 2

CHAPTER 10

THE BEGINNING OF THE END

The fields behind, in front, to the left and right were infinite and knew no beginning or end. Nature, uninterrupted, thrived with untold potential, free from human interference.

Traversing the high hills of the Cotopaxi province in the early hours of the morning, Whalina kept to herself and wondered about the insignificance of human life to nature. *What is a tree without being cut? It is a tree that will grow several feet high. What is a rose without being smelled? It is a rose, living under its own laws. What is a wild hare without penetrating gunshots travelling through the air? It is a hare that may indeed remain prey to a neighbouring animal, prey to the natural cycle of life. Yet what is a human life without nature? Without bees dedicating their lives to pollinate various plants, flowers, and herbs for humanity's survival and pleasure, life is colourless and dull. What is the worth of a human life without the warm rays of sunshine or the cleansing rain? What is the meaning of life if one cannot enjoy the fresh ocean breeze or the freedom of walking barefoot upon the cool ground?* Although taken for granted, nature could never become insignificant to human life. These fields existed before Whalina had been born and will continue to be here long after she will draw her last breath.

The second day of the three-day hike began with them taking the wrong turn, costing an extra hour of walking. The initial beginners' luck and enthusiasm was wearing, and pitying thoughts were fostering with the challenge of the steep ascent.

Whalina stopped under a tall tree and held onto its rough bark. "Neal, wait. I need a break." After throwing the heavy backpack on the ground, she sat in the shade with her back against the supporting tree.

"Everything all right, Al?" Neal knelt to meet her eyes.

"Yes, fine. I think I'm just a little tired."

Neal rummaged through his bag and retrieved a bright red apple.

The smell of food invited a small, stray dog, who lay by Whalina's feet and watched her bite into the crunchy apple. Ecuador was full of stray dogs, and even in the seemingly isolated places, a few were always roaming around with their tongues hanging out. The empty streets of Sigchos, the third village they had now passed, was no exception.

"I thought you slept well last night," Neal said, then bit into a sandwich.

"Like the dead." Whalina gave the apple's core to the four-legged friend to finish.

The small, black dog devoured the core and, with sullen eyes, whimpered softly.

"I don't have any more. Ask Neal."

Neal gave the dog the last piece of his sandwich and pulled Whalina onto her feet.

The day was young. With over ten kilometres to cross before reaching the next hostel in Chugchilán and with limited water and food, it was best to stop only when it was essential. Their destination was the Quilotoa Loop, recommended as one of the top ten things to do in Ecuador. The self-guided, two to three-day hike in the Andes mountains begins or ends at the magnificent Quilotoa Lake. The water-filled caldera had formed eight hundred years ago with a violent volcanic eruption. The views from just under four thousand metres above the crater were one of a kind.

It was their second day of walking through hills and mountains without phone reception, relying solely on old paper maps and intuition for guidance. They had crossed roughly half of the trails' distance and had no choice but to keep going forward, hoping to stay on track and reach their hostel before sunset. The following morning, they planned to set out again, and at the end of that day, the promised Quilotoa Lake would reveal itself.

With the breath-taking view in mind, Whalina marched on with a throbbing headache and several foot blisters, which kept her a few feet behind Neal. Naturally stubborn, she was not one to give up or give in. The fresh mountain air supplemented the much-needed energy, and the penetrating sun motivated her to push on.

The journey itself was beautiful. Perhaps the time spent on the trail would later become more memorable than the destination. Butterflies of all colours and patterns accompanied the trek, and birds sang, knowing no fear or worry of their fate concluding with a face-to-face meeting with a hawk or an eagle. It was unavoidable that every so often, they would stop to admire the view. Each viewpoint was unique and could not be compared to the one that came before or after.

Nature, just like humanity, is unique and original. A flower does not compare itself to other flowers; it just blooms. Humans, too, should not compete with each other; they are all special and beautiful. Without exception, every peak and downhill path was impeccably created, trees scattered in a picturesque formation across the open land, and the never-ending horizon carried a sense of prosperity.

"Stop." Whalina's hazel eyes squeezed shut as she pressed her hand over her chest. Inside, a battle of polarities was tearing her lungs apart; with each breath, a glacier fire was simultaneously freezing and exploding her soul.

Hearing the feeble voice across the small distance between them, Neal turned back to see Whalina hunched forward, holding her chest, and knew to run back.

"What's going on? What's hurting you?" He caught her body in his arms seconds before it hit the ground and carefully placed her head on his knees.

"I can't see. My eyes are not working. Darkness is swallowing me," Whalina uttered out of breath, and Neal watched her wild eyes as they fearlessly stared at the sun. "I see black. Help me, please," she managed to choke out before closing her eyes.

"Ali, stay with me. Speak to me."

Whalina held her breath to stop the pain from spreading. It worked for a moment, but soon after, she was desperate for air and drew a slow, shallow breath. Agony rippled like ocean waves through her chest. Unable to scream without oxygen in her lungs, she drowned in pain.

Neal touched the pale, small palms crossed at the chest. They were ice cold. Time ceased to exist as Whalina's chest stopped moving, and Neal's heart dropped to his stomach. "No, no, no! You're not dying on me again!"

After placing Whalina's head on the ground as quickly and gently as his shaking hands would allow, he ripped her baby-blue t-shirt in half and brought the dull, still body into light. Having seen resuscitation scenes only in films, he had no guarantee that what he was about to do would work, but with no other choice, he placed the heel of his hand and interlaced fingers in the centre of Whalina's chest. With each second holding the possibility of being the defining moment, he had no time to think.

Just before pushing on her chest, Neal took one last look at her face, and just then, her eyes shot open. He did not recognize the woman behind the enlarged dark pupils; the hazel colour was gone, and in its place were large black embers. Whalina's body lay motionless, hosting a set of eyes engraved with deep pain and wisdom. The foreign eyeballs moved lazily from Neal's face to gaze skywards.

The humid air finally let loose, and heavy rain poured from the grey clouds. The restorative waters punctured through her open eyes. A cocktail of tears and rain overflowed, and finally, the murky embers surrendered and closed. Between shallow breaths, Neal saw Whalina's chest rise and fall again; she had not left him. As abruptly as it had arrived, the rain stopped, and as though nothing had happened, the sun emerged from the clouds. The warm light passed through the thin skin on Whalina's eyelids, bringing her awareness to the light, which she thought had been lost. Neal interlaced his fingers with hers. Whalina opened her mouth, trying to find words, but nothing came out.

"Shh, it's okay, Ali. Don't say anything. I'm here. I'm here, darling." The hazel eyes which he had fallen in love with slowly opened. A smile appeared on his face, and for a moment, he forgot all that had just happened.

With caution, Whalina drew a deep breath, which landed her consciousness back into her physical body. "I think I fainted."

The declaration, without sense of concern or worry, bounced off Neal. "I think we should stop the hike."

Whalina analysed Neal's expression—fear. He was afraid to continue.

"It's closer to return to the hostel, and from there, we can get a donkey ride to town," he said, throwing her deeper into the direction of resistance.

Determined to keep going and see the lake, for the blisters that had accumulated on her feet to count for something, Whalina knew turning back was not an option. "Why? I feel better. I can breathe." She turned on all fours to get to her feet. The seemingly instant recovery of her body, that had collapsed and stopped breathing only moments ago, was now in full spirit and eager to press on with the hike.

"Yes, but you stopped breathing just minutes before." Neal's stern voice reminded Whalina of Edward, the same tone her father would use when he would parent her; although harsh, there was love and care behind it.

"I've had trouble breathing ever since I arrived in Ecuador." The warmth of Neal's body was comforting as she wrapped her arms around his waist. "It must be the altitude," she whispered.

"But why didn't you say something before?" With every word that came from his mouth, Neal tightened his arms around her.

"Because I didn't want you to worry." Omitting other elements of the larger truth, Whalina hoped Neal would believe her. Indeed, the burning chest pains made breathing difficult, and although they had been troubling her for some time, only in Ecuador did they become unbearable, forcing her to pay attention. Whalina also pushed aside the insight that sleep had become more of a necessity than food, and if Neal opened her backpack, the antipyretic pills that were helping combat her persistent fevers would fall out.

"Come on, now. We tell each other everything. I love you and need to know when something is wrong." Neal cupped Whalina's face with his palms and wiped the tears off her face. "My baby." He pulled her closer as she cried for reasons she could not understand.

Like many riddles of life, the reality of each individual is independent of another. Created in the mind, the same experience can appear different, depending on the previous experiences. Whilst Whalina released tears of guilt and shame for the secrets that had become a burden to keep, Neal asked how he could help with her altitude sickness. Unwilling to face the consequences of sharing the whole truth, she convinced herself that her symptoms were unrelated and temporary. For now, it was easier to live with the beautiful lie that her body was fighting a simple battle with a cold, which would become wholly insignificant and forgotten in a few days or weeks.

Whalina convinced Neal that turning back would not only be a waste of time, but also effort. The whole first day and a great chunk of the second would be good for nothing. The kilometres crossed on foot, the sweat dripping from their foreheads, and each small victory as they lost and found their path again would now be in vain, so they pushed onwards.

The sun hid behind the grey clouds, and the rest of the hike seemed to be more downhill. Perhaps Mother Nature had a unique pair of eyes and could see past Whalina's pretty lies. Maybe she could hear the whispers of the human souls that passed by. She was always so generous and kind, helping in any way she could. The gentle breeze was helping to keep the hikers cool and to lower her fever. Relieved, Whalina smiled.

"What are you smiling about?" Neal responded with a smile of his own.

"I'm happy to be here with you," she said, grabbing his hand.

With radiant smiles, they continued on the path ahead, truly in the now, without a worry or care for what was to come. The present moment was all they had; it was and always would be the only real thing in life. Even memories were something the human brain constructed—ghosts of the past.

After many hours, remote in the wild and away from familiar life, at last they experienced the raw emotion of pure joy when seeing the large sign reading, Cloud Nine Hostel. Situated between two grand mountains, the building was made with a combination of red bricks and wood. Colourful flags hung from the balconies, and blue and yellow flowerpots populated the ground. It was a happy place, filled with youthful spirit. For some guests, a warm shower and a homemade meal was all that was needed to feel rejuvenated.

Whalina, on the other hand, felt the exhaustion on a whole other level. Besides a few new blisters and aching pain in her legs, which were expected, after all, it was her mind that was most distressed. Unable to focus through a thick brain fog, to concentrate and follow through with a thought, Whalina had no willpower to eat or shower.

"I'll bring some food up for you," Neal said, sitting on the bed beside her.

Whalina wanted to tell him not to worry, that she would be asleep by the time he returned, but her lips and closed eyes were not at her command.

"How are you feeling? You look hot." He shook his head, feeling the heat radiating from her sunburnt forehead.

Whalina peeked through one eye and saw him disappear into the bathroom.

"And you said it wouldn't come in handy." After what seemed like eternity, he returned and placed a small, wet towel over her head.

"Thank you," she murmured and curved her lips into a soft smile.

"Are you sure you don't want to see a doctor?"

Whalina could see the worry on his face and was on the edge of telling him the truth that, indeed, perhaps she did need help, but instead, she just shook her head.

"I'll be as quick as I can. I love you." Neal kissed her forehead and went to have dinner alone.

Whalina was neither asleep nor awake as she floated between her conscious and unconscious mind. She could hear Neal opening the door but was unwilling to open her eyes.

Before losing access to all her senses, she heard Neal say, "Sarah, it's me Neal. Something is happening with Al. Call me."

Whalina fought the wave of sleep, but the master of dreams was stronger, and she was no longer in control of her body.

*****

The sound of crashing glass, in the early hours of the morning, broke the near-total silence and naive peace of the night. The bathroom door was slightly ajar, and wrapped in a towel, Whalina stood in front of the scattered broken pieces. "I'm sorry. I was holding it, and then I wasn't." The words raced out of her mouth as Neal appeared, wide awake, by her side.

"Don't move." He hurriedly put on his walking boots to carry her over the sharp glass. "Ali, you're shaking!" Neal sounded alarmed, even more so than the night before.

Whalina studied her jerky fingers. She felt unstable, and her legs wobbled. "I think I just need to eat something."

"Sit down, baby. I'll get you something. Just wait here a moment."

The door slammed shut, and Whalina heard his heavy boots hit the wooden stairs, then silence. She was alone. A mirror in front of the bed displayed her reflection. She looked radiant with her skin glowing, nothing like the night before. Yet she still felt as though her insides were rotting. Unaware of the lifeforce leaking from her body, Whalina slowly ate breakfast, and despite Neal telling her to rest, she was determined to step outside.

The gentle sunrays kissed her skin, and the air felt moist with life. She took a deep breath and felt the lost energy return to her. The colours looked brighter, and the sound of tree leaves dancing in the wind sounded vibrant and clear. Whalina felt her legs stand strong. She managed to convince Neal to continue their hike, and with heavy backpacks, they set out into the wild. The weather was rooting for their eventual arrival at the lake, and the journey was made pleasant with no rain and the scorching sun hidden.

After getting lost and only having to turn back once, they still felt the day was going according to plan. Conversation flowed more today than the previous two days, although pleasant, about nothing in particular that would later be remembered. The path was at times steep, and then silence would stretch between them as they focused on the placement of their feet and carefully avoided falling through the unguarded open spaces.

At last, they entered the belly of a giant cloud, where everything was white and misty. Together, they walked blindly through the cloud, when, gradually and then all at once, the lake unveiled, and the turquoise lagoon was unlike anything they had seen. A pool of crystal water, surrounded by ancient land, beckoned its spectators through the many narrow valleys that led to the crater. It was a surreal feeling to be immersed in the fog whilst surveying the edges of the time-worn extinct volcano. What they saw could never be contained in a picture frame or made just, even with a thousand words. The energy of the lava which used to flow over the land more than eight hundred years ago still pulsated through the ground, delivering an influx of goosebumps. Natives believed the lake was bottomless and continued through to the infinity of its depth, eventually leading to the Earth's centre.

Overlooking the entire lake, Whalina kneeled and allowed the most untampered scene of beauty take her breath away. It had been an emotional and challenging three-day journey, but the Quilotoa Lake was worth every bit of tears and sweat. The refreshing breeze washed over Whalina's face and silently cleansed her skin. The ancient volcano's energy rushed through her body, and she felt the divine circulate inside her veins. In this moment of release, the truth was no longer staying buried, and she knew something greater than life itself was coming. There was nothing left to do but accept the fate destined for her. Whalina had never been so happy before; it was unlike anything human she had ever experienced. She finally felt the journey home was coming to an end, and the possibility of feeling whole and complete, just the way she was, could be possible. Although, she did not know why or how she knew the end of the life she had lived was ending and a new beginning was just around the corner.

They stayed a while, sitting a bit from the edge, and enjoyed the simplicity of the moment.

*****

Walking down the walls of the crater, Whalina reminisced about the wonderful views she had shared with Sarah and Neal on top of the grand mountain at the end of the TelefériQo ride. That day, they had been about to take the ride back into town, when the clouds changed their mind and opened a window, displaying the city of Quito from one side and behind the active Pichincha Volcano. It had been as though a greater power moved the clouds so they would not leave without seeing what Earth had to offer. She wondered whether a higher consciousness had moved the clouds that day and if it was the same creator who had fed her the strength to finish the hike today.

Surrounded by the walls of the crater, Whalina was steps from the captivating shoreline, when a knot tightened inside her chest. She bent down and reached her hand, but instead of touching the sublime water, the familiar darkness returned. As she walked blindly through a thick tarlike field, no one heard Whalina's scream. When the dark, murky eyes opened, the deep, open waters were revealed, and Whalina's conscious mind and soul were locked inside the body of a whale.

CHAPTER 11

ONE SOUL, TWO BODIES

The dream and waking world merged. Despite Whalina's eyes being opened, her mind believed that the unfamiliar room she was in was nothing more than a vivid dream. The colours appeared brighter and more vibrant than ever, especially the thin trees outside the enormous glass window. They were neon green, reminding her of a treasured childhood memory where she and Sarah had painted their faces using the green pigmentation of leaves.

The sound of innocence, carried in on a child's laugh, brought a warm, fuzzy feeling to her body and a deep longing to feel the naive and carefree nature of a child again. The laughter became louder and clearer, making Whalina wonder whether the child was real or a figment of her imagination. It would be wonderful if it was real, she thought, and imagined curly golden locks on a little girl's head. The image created in her mind stood in front of her as the bright spirals bounced with ease; like a little lamb, she ran, playing a game of tag. Whalina playfully tackled the child and tickled her, infecting herself with the untamed, contagious laughter. Stuck between wakefulness and sleep, Whalina clung to the little girl as though she was the future and followed her until they reached the Quilotoa Lake. It was as beautiful and enchanting as the first time.

Mesmerising and promising, the crystal-clear turquoise water was inviting, and the golden-locked girl tried to release her hand from Whalina's tightening grip. Determined to keep her from the cunning lake, Whalina carried the small body into the jungle. The child's cry sucked the neon colour from the trees and turned the leaves into a dull, lifeless brown. The dying trees fell, carving a pathway behind Whalina and the young girl she was trying to tame. The wicked cry wrecked all that stood in their way, and although she wanted to save her, Whalina realised her love was suffocating the child. If she loved her, she had to give up and let her go.

She watched the little person run determinedly though the destroyed jungle towards the lake and disappear into the water. Saddened by the loneliness and loss of hope, Whalina turned from the lake and found herself where she thought it had begun: in the unknown room facing the enormous window and the shining neon trees outside.

A sudden twitch in her left leg brought her attention to her physical body, which she had forgotten. Wilfully, her toes wiggled, and Whalina believed that what she had just seen had been a dream. This was the waking world. Curious to see the other half of the unknown room, Whalina slowly rolled from facing the window and onto her back.

On the other half of the bed slept Sarah, curled into a ball, wearing long white pants and a loose white shirt. The red string bracelet with a golden heart, a gift from Whalina for Sarah's eighteenth birthday, was wrapped tightly around her wrist.

"Are you real?" Whalina whispered and touched the metal heart, finding it warm after absorbing Sarah's body heat. Wanting more of the radiating glow, Whalina gently stroked her sister's face, feeling its warmth.

"Whally …" Sarah rolled over.

Finding that no words could express the extremity of what needed to be said, they remained silent, studying each other as if they were memorising each other's features.

At times, the simplicity of another's presence or physical closeness is enough to carry the weight of a thousand words. There are certain circumstances where even a stranger could fill the void, despair, and confusion of a human soul, where nothing but presence and silence is the most healing methodology. A seemingly simple hug or the sound of another beating heart can take away the pain of a bullet.

"Whally, how are you feeling?"

And with just one question, the pain can be brought back.

Knowing her grip on reality was fading, Whalina ran out of places to hide and was afraid that her time would soon also run out.

"Is Neal here?" she asked, knowing he too deserved to know the truth.

"Yes, and there's one other person I would like you to meet." Sarah left, leaving the doors open.

Whalina slowly looked around, beholding the new surroundings. The walls and floors were made from dark wood so shiny that Whalina ran her hand over the wall behind the bed to feel the smooth, impeccable texture. The grand window ensured the room was well lit, bringing everything to light. Whalina felt an immediate sense of release as she saw Neal walk through the door.

The two had a moment to themselves before Sarah promptly returned with a tall man, also dressed in white, with very long, tied-back black hair.

"Whally, this is Wind. He is my friend and shaman." Sarah sat on the bed next to Whalina, and Wind slid a chair closer. She felt clammy and had the urge to shower.

"Nice to meet you, Wind," Whalina said purely from politeness, for she could not understand why Sarah thought it was a good idea to meet the stranger right now. Expecting an old indigenous man with red paint on his face and a feather, she was intimidated and uneasy around the shaman.

The beautiful, young man fixated on her, and she eyed Neal, who met her with a reassuring smile.

"You are not from here," the shaman said, breaking the silence. His English was surprisingly good, and his voice was assertive. Whalina thought he was being arrogant, asking a question he surely already knew the answer to.

"No, I'm from England." Then she realised Wind had not asked a question but had simply stated the obvious. The intensity of his eye contact was unnerving, and Whalina looked to Sarah, hoping for a miraculous telepathic explanation to why she had brought him here.

Sarah placed her hand over Whalina's and squeezed it.

"Why are you here?" Wind had a strong Spanish accent and spoke calmly, which only made Whalina more nervous.

Feeling like a child on the edge of getting in trouble, she did not like the confident tone and the way he spoke. She had been conditioned to the tedious Western customs of communication, and the shaman's direct nature and refusal to use the social buffers she had become accustomed to had thrown her. She wanted to answer with, *"I am well, thank you, and how are you?"* But instead, she decided to play his game. "In Ecuador or here? Because I don't even know where here is." Whalina felt attacked and wanted Wind to leave.

"Why are you here?" he repeated in the same calm and monotonous voice.

"Because I came here on holiday. I wanted to see Sarah." She glared at her sister with her eyes yelling, *Save me! Who is this strange man?*

"It's okay, Whally. Just tell him the truth." Sarah offered another one of her reassuring looks.

Confronted by eyes all around her and the illuminating light from the window, Whalina had nowhere to hide. "I don't know what you're talking about, Sarah."

"I think we should give Al some time to rest," Neal said to Sarah, who completely ignored him.

"Whally, have you been experiencing anything out of the ordinary? Unusual, unexplainable recently? Please just tell us the truth so we can help."

Whalina's head throbbed with an oncoming migraine, and she had no strength to fight her sister, so she surrendered.

"We had a car accident a month ago, and since then, I have been feeling a little out of place." Whalina addressed Wind whilst looking at Neal, wanting him to confirm the story and take her side. "Maybe things were not quite right before the accident, too. Shadows and strange dreams. I don't know when it really started," she added, feeling somewhat guilty. The signs were there, but she didn't pay attention.

The shaman answered immediately, as though he knew what she would say and had his words pre-written and ready to be spoken. "Would you not say it's normal to feel out of place after a traumatic experience like that?"

Cornered, Whalina understood the workings of this man and his unique way of communication. Walking out from under the shadows, Whalina felt a blockage inside her throat. She took a deep breath and swallowed saliva down to her gut, then opened up in front of the strange man. "After the accident, I felt more out of place than ever before and knew something needed to change. I came to Ecuador, hoping to find myself and my place in the world. To feel peace, maybe belong to something." She paused, hearing the words echo. Time seemed to slow as a wave of clarity engulfed and lifted a weight off her shoulders.

"A place I was under the illusion that I had. But now I don't even have that. The illusion is gone, and I feel the gaps inside, holes I can no longer deny or attempt to fill." Whalina had crossed the bridge of no return; when one admits a deep truth out loud, it can no longer hold down the truth-seeker.

Wind smiled as though he had finally gotten what he was searching for.

"Now, can someone tell me what happened?" Whalina asked, without directing the question to anyone in particular.

Neal recounted the events, starting from when she had lost consciousness at the lake. Sarah had already heard Neal's voicemail from the night before, and together, with Wind, they had travelled to Quilotoa. Neal had told Sarah, who had shared the news with Wind, about Whalina's behaviour and the dark, murky eyes she had become a host to. Wind seemed confident he knew the symptoms, and the loss of colour in her eyes suggested only one thing, yet he would not say what. Neal had taken some persuasion, but eventually, he gave in and trusted Sarah, who, in turn, trusted the shaman.

They took Whalina to Wind's house in the Amazon jungle, where they spent several hours working with her spirit, willing her soul to return. Whalina did not know it yet, but the shaman knew her better than she knew herself. With no recollection of where her soul had wandered to or what it had experienced, Whalina had no idea how far she had ventured outside her body.

"Is that what you wanted me to say?" she asked the shaman, feeling a gaping sadness which he knew too well, having met her soul.

"You only just met me, but for this to work, you must trust me. I've been working with your sister for the past few months, and we have now become friends. I do not wish harm upon your path." Wind spied Sarah, who met his gaze.

"Whally, Wind is a good man and a trusted friend, one I trust with my life. You don't need to be afraid. Please let him help you—"

"Help me with what, exactly?" Whalina pulled herself up on the bed. "What the hell happened to me?" She saw Neal looking at the floor, then she noticed the light had dimmed from Sarah's eyes; for the second time in her life, she was truly afraid. Perhaps even more afraid when she had believed death was near and that she was on the edge of drowning in the accident. Whenever a dark cloud had followed her in the past, it was Sarah and Neal who would hold the umbrella, but today, they were emptyhanded.

Whatever forces were at play, she was on the losing team and, deep down, knew Wind was the only one who could save her.

*****

WIND – FORTY-EIGHT HOURS BEFORE

When Whalina arrived in the jungle, her spiritual state was critical, and there was no time to waste. Neal needed to hear that traditional medicine could do very little to bring Whalina back into a conscious state, and so they summoned a trusted medical doctor, who confirmed her physical body was in a stable condition. Her blood pressure was normal, and there was no sign of physical distress, only that it was impossible to wake her up. Neal agreed to give Wind a chance, but if the shaman's way did not work, Sarah supported his decision, and they would take Whalina to the best hospital in the capital. For now, they placed all their trust in Wind and his shamanic knowledge to retrieve Whalina from wherever her soul had wandered to.

The shaman's great-grandfather had taught him, and he had several years of experience working in the spirit realm. The shamanic cosmology is a world filled with spiritual beings; energies, spirit guides, angels, ancestors, totem animals, gods, goddesses, and nature spirits all reside there. It is those helpful spirits who guide the human consciousness towards healing and wisdom in the human world. When one feels lost and disconnected from the self, a shamanic ritual can help guide them home to themselves. One of the great missions of shamanic work is to help heal the soul, known as the vital essence of an individual. A shaman works to restore spiritual power to the physical body and resolve any physical, mental, or emotional issues.

From the moment Wind set his eyes on Whalina, he could see she was nothing but an empty shell of a body. Before him was a vessel which used to home a soul; the living essence of what made a person real was gone. He called her condition a *spiritual coma* and explained that the only way for Whalina to return would be to do a soul-retrieval ceremony. The shaman admitted that usually only fragments of the soul would be missing and there was no guarantee Whalina's soul would return. Without being able to communicate with her human parts, they may already be too late. She may have wandered too far into the spiritual cosmos, seeking her lost parts.

Seeing that Sarah believed Wind and how she saw him as the answer to saving her sister, Neal agreed to the ceremony. Under usual circumstances, the person whose soul had been fragmented would be awake, and a pool of communication would take place between the shaman and the participant. In this case, Wind had to improvise and asked Sarah and Neal to share what they thought were Whalina's most fond and treasured memories. It was important that it was not their memories with Whalina but what they believed she held closest to her heart. Neal shared a picture of Whalina's unfinished painting and the story of how much the completion of the artwork meant to her. Sarah believed her sister was happiest when in water and talked about Whalina's love of the sea.

The soul-retrieval ceremony took place on the same evening as soon as the sun had set. Wind called his younger brother Icaro, also a shaman, to help facilitate the process. Icaro's role seemed simple yet imperative in helping Wind enter a shamanic trance. Icaro was in his twenties and no more than five feet tall. He had the great responsibility of playing the drums. The specific rhythm and pace would enable Wind to enter the desired brainwave, which would correspond to the relevant spiritual energy centres vibrating in response. The physical and mental body were of no use here; all that mattered was the subtle energetic body which would be used as a conveyance for transportation between the human and spiritual world.

Sarah and Neal sat at the top of the circle, with a small fire between them that helped illuminate Whalina's way home, who lay in the centre. An intention to guide Whalina's soul into her human body was set, and Icaro began drumming. The fast beating of the drum never changed rhythm, and soon Wind stood with one foot in the spiritual realm and the other on Earth.

Humans often lose parts of their soul due to trauma or because of unimaginable spiritual pain. The broken part of the soul will wait to be reunited with the other half of the soul, who, in turn, yearns in agony to be whole again. Very soon, he realised Whalina's fragmented soul was not in the realm of time and space where he believed she had been existing. Usually, we are reincarnated with our whole soul intact, and throughout the many ups and downs of life, parts of the soul may chip away. This was not the case with Whalina, whose entire soul had wandered beyond the realm of life on Earth.

Wind envisioned the painting of the mysterious woman Neal had described and imagined holding a wooden paintbrush. After feeling pleasure and relief of finding the right colour, Wind finally let the brush meet the empty part of the canvas. A vivid image of a girl with golden locks blew towards him on a wave of ice-cold air. The penetrating cold made his body shiver as he watched the girl stand in front of the painting.

She looked into the blank space surrounding the cream-coloured ceramic walls adorned with a beautiful painted pattern of purple flowers and dark green leaves. As though a grand idea sparked her mind, she faced the canvas and mixed the paints. The beautiful girl did not bear any resemblance to the Whalina that Wind knew, yet he was certain it was her soul that stood before him. The sound of his chattering teeth broke the image into several tiny pieces. The glass-filled floor turned into a thick smoking tar beneath his feet.

With Whalina's face imprinted in his mind's eyes, Wind ran through the burning ground, until the blazing fire encircled him with no escape. By using the combination of powerful thought and emotion, Wind was heading exactly where he needed to be. The visual picture of the sea and Whalina blended with the feeling of relief at finishing the painting, creating an opening in the fire, leading Wind down a portal into a foreign realm. Wind's soul emerged through the seabed of a dark ocean. Unlike the waters on Earth, this place was bleak and deeply melancholy.

All around were falling clusters of black tar from above, which came in different shapes and sizes; some pieces were shapeless and heavy, whilst others resembled the frame of various human body parts. A small sphere with a round indent floated down and brushed over Wind's spirit. A flashback memory revealed the indent was a formation of an open mouth screaming from pain. The falling tar pieces were all parts of various souls, once whole but now broken and spread across the vast ocean waters.

Wind knew the dangers of letting the pool of agonising souls distract him and refocused on finding Whalina, his anchor to both this world and the one he came from. With the anchor in mind, he swam through another mournful site, a cemetery of unsettled skeletons and rotting fish. It was a dead zone not only for marine life, but also for humans, whose bones cracked in half and rattled as Wind's white soul swam by. They yelled and cried for him to stop and help, but Wind knew he'd be risking getting trapped and lost himself. The lost souls must have endured great agony and died a tragic death. Unable to move on and heal, they were stuck in the in-between of being dead in a world of the living.

Feeling that life was near, Wind pushed on with determination and purpose, as the longer Whalina remained in the cold waters of the dead, the more damage would be inflicted on her soul—damage which may result in her already fragmented self to disintegrate even further, diminishing any chance of her return to her physical body back on Earth. With profound misery and torment engraved by the energy of this place, Whalina's weakened soul would see no future beyond this realm.

The water grew warmer, and Wind thought he saw a small light shining ahead. Following the light, he swam forward, burning away the dark spirits who tried to attach themselves to his bright soul. Wind's spirit had thousands of years of practice and training; his present reincarnation was not the first, and in many ways, his soul knew how to repel dark energies.

The light ahead brightened, and the illuminating creature was finally clear. Wind came face to face with a giant blue whale. It was here that life was most present; he knew it was Whalina's fluorescent light that made the whale shine so bright. Wind looked deeply into the whale's murky eyes and saw the fear and loss of Whalina's entrapped soul. The animal was feeding off Whalina's essence; she had been his life source since before he had been born. Wind could not understand how one soul could exist in two separate realms, leading two entirely different lives and realities—a human life and a whale's existence, totally separate yet inherently intertwined.

A broken soul would always gravitate towards its missing half; thus, the two lives would always be inseparable. Wind wondered what that meant for Whalina and if it was possible she was born with only one-half of her soul.

Wind had questions which he knew only Whalina could answer and communicated with the half of the soul he knew as Whalina. "Whalina, you must return home. You must complete your life purpose." Wind chose his words carefully, for he did not know how deeply Whalina had become rooted in the realm of the whale.

"This is my home. It's what I've always been looking for," he heard Whalina's voice in his head. Wind could see that although the two halves of her soul were inside the whale, the merge had not yet taken place, which meant it was still possible for her to return.

"You feel loss and fear. This cannot be home. Home is love, and there is no love in this place," Wind tried to plead with her, but Whalina remained in a trance. The two souls could merge at any time, becoming one soul; if that happened, Whalina would never return home to Earth. Wind had to take a different approach. "Neal. You blew air into his lungs and brought him back to life. Remember that?"

Grief poured from the luminescent soul, and Wind knew he was poking her where it hurt the most.

"He is waiting for you. You can come back here, but you must say goodbye first."

The blue whale opened its gigantic mouth and released a high-frequency whistle. The piercing sound reached hundreds of miles underwater and shook the ocean bed, exhuming all that was lifeless and dead and throwing it into the desert of the deep waters. The polluted waters became a traffic of dead matter and dark spirits. Before Wind could say anything else, the whale banged his heavy tail through the water current and swam away with fury.

Buried in the gaping mouth of darkness with energy-sucking spirits attaching themselves to his spirit, Wind was forced to venture back. Searching for the sound of the beating drums which would lead him home, Wind closed his eyes until the rhythm returned. The drumming grew louder until finally Wind's spirit was reunited with his physical body. The sky was a blend of light and dark; dawn was a sacred time in the jungle.

Wind never returned from a soul retrieval empty-handed. He always came back bearing the sweet fragment of a relieved soul that was grateful to be reunited and made whole. However, Whalina's soul was no ordinary soul, and this was unlike any journey he had ever been on. Instead of restoring the fragmented soul, he gently blew his breath into Whalina's heart centre, knowing she would need all the strength and protection she could get.

CHAPTER 12

THE RIVER OF LIFE

"So, if half of my soul is still out there, how did I make it back and wake up?" she asked Wind.

"I believe your soul remembered your life on Earth. But I must be honest, this is new to me too." The Shaman looked almost sad.

Having never felt so powerless, Whalina wanted to wake up from the never-ending nightmare and wished for things to return to the way they had been before the accident.

"We need to go back to the very beginning," he interrupted her negative thought spiral.

"Is all of this happening because of the accident and the vision of that woman?" she asked, sitting upright on the wooden bed.

"From what I understood, the woman told you to go home. She knew your soul and that you were not from here. It was always your destiny to go home—home being the other realm." Wind looked down, as though there was more to the story that he was not telling.

"How much time do I have until I lose myself again?" Whalina asked with the three pairs of eyes approaching from all directions.

Silence filled the room as its occupants dreaded hearing the answer.

"It could be minutes, hours, or days. The workings of your peculiar case are not quite understood." Wind had taken it upon himself to answer, for both Sarah and Neal looked clueless.

Unable to meet the gaze of another, Whalina's crystal eyes focused on the pure white sheets.

"I know this is a lot to take in, Whally," Sarah said, "but—"

Whalina waved a clear stop command in front of her face. "Leave me alone, please. I'm tired, and I don't want to hear anymore." Whalina briefly met Sarah's eyes before closing hers to save the tears from falling. The sisters rarely argued, and when they did, it was always over something trivial.

Sarah looked to Neal for guidance, who gestured with a gentle nod that it was best to leave. Wind walked outside, and Sarah followed, closing the door behind her.

Whalina's mind was blown by Wind's relay of the spiritual journey he had undertaken to save her soul. A death penalty had been sentenced, one which she knew very little about and had no idea when it would commence.

"You too, Neal, please go," Whalina uttered with closed eyes, failing to stop the escaping tears from streaking her face.

"I'm not going anywhere. I'll never leave you." Neal tried to cradle her into his arms, but she pulled away.

She didn't want his touch. She didn't want to infect him with her sadness. "I mean it. I need to be alone." She bit her lip so the tears stayed at bay.

"We always get through things together, Ali, and this is no different. I'm here for you. Forever and always."

Whalina knew he meant it, and just like that, he broke down her walls.

"I'm so scared. I don't want to die." Finally letting herself feel, she cried like a feral animal. The loud whimpering ricocheted off Neal's chest back into Whalina's body.

He cupped her soft face into his palms. "You are not dying, Al. Over my dead body will I part from you. There's always a way; we will find a way."

Her mournful cry continued as she finally acknowledged and released the pent-up fear that had been fostering inside her since before she was born. Whalina lived an entire lifetime feeling misunderstood, different, and never truly belonging, it finally made sense, and she knew Wind was telling the truth. Yet knowing she had been right all along did not make her heart any lighter. A life of beautiful ignorance and bliss had served her in ways she now knew she had taken for granted. Having another being confirm something was extraordinary about her did not make life easier.

"Why did this happen to me? Why can't I just be normal?" Whalina sobbed, unaware of how potent her emotions and energy were.

*****

WIND

Wind, who was in the room next door, could sense the ancient, vibrating sorrow penetrating through his skin. The young girl and her immense power, which had lived inside her for many lifetimes, fascinated him. In his many years of practice, he had never encountered a human being so powerful—a human who had survived so long with half their soul in another dimension, providing the life energy for the greatest marine mammal in history. The whale was symbolic of that which would not be vanquished silently; it cannot be subdued or silenced, just like the voice of truth found in the soul.

Could it be that Whalina's soul chose the whale as a method of preservation for her own soul? Wind was scratching his head, knowing the answers they sought were already unmasked in Whalina's subconscious mind. The obstacle ahead was the girl and her own resistance to surrender and to come through in a vulnerable state, ready to face herself. It was as though Wind's thoughts had the ability to influence Whalina's state of mind, and she had finally stopped the tears from flowing.

*****

WHALINA

"Can I ask you something?" She delayed the delivery of the real question and held her breath.

"Of course, Al. Anything," he responded faster than she had wanted and gently held her hand almost as though he could sense what she was thinking.

"If I die—"

Neal tried to interrupt before she could say another word.

"Please allow me to say this. If I die, you must promise to live your very best life. Don't mourn and be sad for too long. Name your first child after me. If I have any say where I go after death, it will be right back home to you." A silent tear escaped and rolled down her puffy face.

"Al, what are you saying, baby?"

"Please just promise me." Her voice strangled, and she looked straight into Neal's eyes.

"Alright, I promise." He wrapped his arms tightly around Whalina's frail body and caressed her head.

Within minutes, she was again fast asleep.

*****

When Whalina awoke, it was pitch dark outside, and Neal was sleeping soundly next to her. Her attention went to the ticking watch on his wrist—which read, 4:44. Panicked, as more time had escaped her grasp, she slowly crept from bed. The cool wooden floor had never felt so good under her feet. She was grateful to be walking, most of all to be in control of where she was walking to, even if it was just the en suite bathroom.

The artificial light momentarily blinded her dark eyes, but the true shock came from the reflection in the mirror. Her face was pale, with dark purple circles under the small, swollen eyes. The once-vibrant red lips were cracked and had lost their colour. Unable to previously appreciate the beauty of her round face and puffy cheeks, today Whalina was saddened to see them go. The weight had not only been lost in her face, but also the thin arms and small thighs. The youthful, childlike beauty, which had never quite been loved nor accepted before, was replaced with the skeleton copy of the body she remembered.

Stepping into the shower with determination to reverse or, at least, mask what could no longer be fixed, she let the warm water run over her feeble body. Astonished that the human body could change so rapidly, she realised she had no idea what day of the week it was. For the first time in her life, Whalina had lost track of time, as though months could have passed since their arrival in Ecuador.

Whalina wondered whether they had missed their flight home, but before getting too engrossed in that possibility, she realised the thought of not going back didn't bother her much. After all, no one and nothing was waiting for her in England; the people who mattered the most were here. Besides, she was beginning to accept that she needed the kind of help that Western medicine was unlikely to provide. The spell of unconsciousness throwing her into a deep coma could return at any moment, and Wind was her only hope for a cure.

Even though her physical features had not changed, Whalina felt refreshed and more like herself after the warm shower. Someone had laid out a pair of clean, white pants and a shirt on the chair in the bedroom. Without clean clothes of her own, Whalina was grateful to whomever had prepared them ahead of time. Unable to find a pair of shoes, she quietly walked out of the bedroom and into a narrow hallway.

Wooden doors lined each side, and at the end, a large glass door led into the garden. Whalina stepped onto the cool soil and took a deep breath, filling her body with the fresh Amazonian air. It was a blend of scents, a cocktail of vegetation, moisture, and soil. It was the smell of life. The door slammed shut, alerting the birds sleeping in the nearby tree. It was dead quiet; even the crickets were dreaming, and the only sound was the flow of a nearby river. The sky was an extraordinary showcase of the deepest purple she had ever seen. The intensity and depth of colour faded with distance and the closely approaching sunrise.

Following the calming sound of the water, Whalina found a stone footpath which led to a small handmade wooden bench positioned a few feet from the riverbank. The Amazon River could not be compared to the magnificent crystal waters of the Quilotoa Lake. The river was a muddy-brown colour, carrying tons of mud and sand with its rapid current. Sitting on the bench, Whalina became mesmerised with the untamed current, a force of nature flowing ruthlessly unafraid. It was unstoppable and on a mission to go wherever it was that rivers must go. For a while, Whalina's thoughts swam away with it. She became no one, existed nowhere, doing nothing, just half a soul floating in the cosmos. Unaware of time passing, a human being simply becomes the now. The joyful sound of birds entered the meditative awareness, reminding Whalina of her being.

When she opened her eyes, she saw Wind sitting by her side. "It is magnificent, isn't it?" he said, staring at the river.

"Yes, it's quite lovely," Whalina answered and immediately wished she had said something more meaningful.

"Are you uncomfortable? Would you rather I leave?" Wind asked without breaking his focus on the river.

Heat spread across Whalina's back, and her palms collected sweat. "I feel intimidated by you," she said without thinking, and before she could give him a chance to respond, she continued, "You seem to know more about me than I do about myself. You read my thoughts and know exactly how I'm feeling without me telling you. The worst thing about it all is that I have no choice but to trust you, because my body is no longer my own." Whalina faced him, longing to meet his eyes.

Wind ignored her heavy breathing and the burning desire for him to see her. Focused on the river, he said, "I cannot read your thoughts. But it is true, I did meet the naked version of you. Don't feel intimidated; you are a beautiful soul." Wind listened to her shallow breath deepen. "The longer you run, resist, or hide, the more you have to lose. You are not broken, Whalina."

She knew exactly what the shaman was referring to. Truthfully, she had run out of places to hide. It was no longer an option to bury herself in work, blend into a crowd, or drown in the monotonous mundane life.

Despite it being a safe, cushioned, comfortable life, it lacked happiness and fulfilment. It was that life which kept her soul's purpose away.

"There is always a choice, Whalina. Sometimes it's the harder choice that is the right one." He allowed her a moment to digest his direct way of communication, then graced her with his eyes. "A charming lie appears easier to swallow than the most brutal of truths, but no one ever talks about the side effects of the beautiful lie."

Whalina looked away from the intense energy radiating from the shaman's eyes and refocused on the water. Without warning, a tree branch fell into the river. The strong current pulled it away, and Whalina realised she no longer wanted to live a lie.

"There you are. I've been looking everywhere for you." Sarah's voice came from behind as she approached. Sarah stopped walking, realising Whalina was not alone. "Sorry, I didn't know you were with Wind. I'll leave you two alone." Slightly flustered, Sarah turned back, and if it was not for the tan, her cheeks would have turned rosy.

"It's quite all right. I better get inside. I have to take care of some things." As swiftly as he had arrived, Wind quickly disappeared between the bushes that led to the house.

Taking his place on the bench, Sarah sat beside Whalina, who was eager to make things right again with her sister.

Whalina took Sarah's hand into her own. "I'm sorry I lost my temper before."

"It's nothing, Whally. Don't worry your pretty mind with that." She smiled humbly.

Curious and eager to discuss anything other than the big elephant in the room, Whalina asked, "What is this place? I cannot hear any cars or people."

Sarah explained that this was where she and Mikey had been volunteering. They would help Wind with organising various plant ceremonies and the overall customer experience. The main lodge where the tourists stayed was within close proximity and the enclosed staff quarters was where they were staying. To arrive at the lodge, one must take a twenty-minute ride in a paddle canoe over the Amazon River, making this a secluded spot of retreat.

"And Wind's family? Where are they?" This hidden part of the world fascinated Whalina.

"Deeper in the jungle. They keep to themselves." Sarah interlaced her arm around Whalina's and came a little closer so their hips touched.

Her face glowed with the excitement of a young child when she said, "I spoke to Mum."

Whalina matched Sarah's glow. Eager to know the details of the conversation, her eyes widened with anticipation.

"The phone rang for several seconds before I picked up, and when I finally did, Mum started a conversation as though nothing had happened." Sarah's voice grew louder, fuelled by raw emotion. "Whally, she asked about Colombia, not to criticise or put me down. She wanted to know how I'm doing." She spoke with pure passion as her face gleamed with naivety and bliss.

Having always felt guilty being Mum's favourite, Whalina was content with the news and the prospect of Teresa extending her unconditional mother's love to Sarah. It was true that their mother was no saint, but if she was one thing, it would be brutally honest. Teresa would never say something just to please another, and the very fact that the good of her will had broken the silent treatment suggested a change of heart.

"Why do you think she called?" Sarah asked, and Whalina knew her little sister wanted confirmation this would last, that Teresa meant well and she was not foolish to get her hopes up.

"I guess she realised her mistake and didn't want to risk losing you." She kissed Sarah's forehead. Whalina felt a sense of relief knowing that no matter what happened to her, her little sister and mother would be just fine.

"I knew we'd find them here." Mikey's deep voice carried through the thick jungle air. He was slender and much taller than Neal, who walked beside him down the hilly path. Just like Sarah, Mikey was a free spirit. They had found each other at a climbing centre in London and quickly began spending all their time together.

"Good morning, ladies. How are we doing on this fine day?" Mikey planted a brief kiss on Sarah's lips, then opened his arms, and Whalina stood to greet him. His short, curly hair smelled of fresh lavender. "Sorry about this, but I need to borrow your sister for a moment, if that's okay?"

The place where Sarah had been sitting became vacant, until Neal sat and wrapped his arm around her waist. The cells of her body danced in response to his touch.

"I feel like I have barely seen you," Whalina said quietly, burying her head on his shoulder.

"I have been by your side every waking and sleeping moment. Until this morning, when you disappeared on me."

Light but genuine laughter came to Whalina with ease. Such is the beauty of love that even in the most grievous of times, the union of two soulmates can give the illusion of the whole world disappearing. The confused mind in turmoil found stillness and enjoyed the simplicity of the present moment. The river was no longer furiously racing to the finish line. Instead, it was gracefully flowing in a beautiful water song.

Neal had always been her haven, a place of retreat where she found clarity and peace. Yet when something is found, it is often the case that something also needs to be lost to restore the balance.

The sun was rising, and with it, new questions surfaced. Although the time spent in Ecuador had felt like eternity, Whalina learnt their three-week holiday was ending, and their flight back to England was tomorrow. She had to make a choice, something Whalina was never good at.

"What should I do?" she asked, fixated on the river.

"That is something only you know, Al." Neal swallowed loudly and quickly added, "You have nothing to lose. Let Wind help you and go into it with an open mind." This was the answer Whalina had been searching for. A confirmation from Neal delivered confidence and allowed for the belief that her intuition was guiding her in the right direction.

The air was warm, and the sun was gently peeking from the blue horizon sky, when the river stole Whalina's attention. As though someone had taken a bath cork from the riverbed, the water level sunk. Standing at the riverbank, Whalina witnessed the once-alive wild flow of water turn into a small stream. Alarmed and deeply saddened by the loss, she turned to alert Neal but found Sacnicte sitting in his place.

Unconcerned by the dying river or Whalina, the white-haired ghost was minding her own business, ripping the petals off a white bell-shaped flower.

"What are you doing here?" Whalina shouted, storming towards the old woman.

Sacnicte slowly lifted her head from the flower and gestured for Whalina to sit beside her. Like the first time they had met on the train, she was wearing a white coat, with golden leaves for buttons, and her thin hair blew to the will of the wind.

"Are you responsible for the river?" Whalina sat on the other side of the bench.

"No, my dear, you are." Sacnicte pulled off the last petal, and Whalina watched it softly land on the ground. "That river represents your life source," Sacnicte confidently announced, then stood. Her wrinkled face was soft but aged, making Whalina feel bad for having shouted at the elderly woman.

Sacnicte began walking away but stopped when she heard Whalina ask, "What are you talking about? Who are you?"

Sighing deeply, Sacnicte turned around. "My dear child, please don't be afraid. He will smell the fear on you. You must be strong now."

Whalina looked at the ground, covered with the white flowers, and saw the black tar footprints that Sacnicte's white shoes had created.

CHAPTER 13

WHAT THE DARKNESS BRINGS WITH HIM

Time: The First Night That Belonged to the Dark
Location: The Fallen Kingdom of Light

When Remedy walked through the door of the marble palace, a strong pungent odour, smelling like the aftermath of a fire, took her by surprise. It wasn't the inviting smell of wood smoke or sage but rather the smell of burning something artificial or a manmade substance. It invoked a feeling of uncertainty, making the place she called home feel foreign, as though an unwanted guest occupied it. Remedy was sure she had come across this smell before but couldn't pinpoint its origin. The candles on the wall were about to perish, and the silent hallway was ill lit.

Remedy stopped at the bottom of the staircase to take notice of her great-grandfather's wooden clock. It was past midnight, and she silently hoped the previous turbulent day and night had finally found its end. Her feet made no sound as she padded towards her parents' bedroom, wishing to find them awake. She pressed her ear against the grand wooden door to listen for signs of movement or conversation. The sound of Mama's favourite record came through the door, a slow instrumental melody composed of violin and harp. The delicate, sweet sound was designed to touch the energetic centre of the heart, and it did just that for Remedy, warming her heart and making her feel a little more comfortable inside. She so wanted to open the door but didn't want to risk waking Mama, for recently she'd had trouble sleeping.

Remedy sat on the cool floor and closed her eyes, knowing that if her parents were awake, they would feel her presence outside their bedroom. Her mind floated into space, with the musical notes playing in the background, drifting between Kai and her grandmother, wondering when and if she'd see either of them again.

All those without a physical body have the power to project themselves into the world of the physical. It can be in the form of light or dark shadows, dreams, or even animals. A soul can also imprint itself into a human's consciousness and appear real in front of them. But for that to happen, there must be a great reason, such as an important message that could alter the destiny of one or many lives. A soul cannot simply return to say any unsaid words and goodbyes, but to die without choice is a violation of free will.

Remedy wondered whether her grandmother could return and reassure her that everything was fine. She wondered whether Sacnicte could see her now, and taking a chance that she could, Remedy whispered, "Grandma, I don't understand what happened. Why didn't you have time to say goodbye?"

She swallowed her tears down and listened attentively, expecting to hear a voice in her head or for the answer to intuitively come to her. Before Sacnicte could possibly answer, Remedy's attention shifted to Papa as he opened the door. Remedy jumped to her feet and hugged him closely. She was expecting to find comfort in the familiar scent Papa carried on him: a blend of geranium and ocean breeze from the hours he spent on the waters. But instead, Remedy was taken aback when she inhaled the familiar but unpleasant smell of the burning fire.

"What is this smell?" She gently pulled away, not wanting to hurt his feelings.

"It must be from the burial fire. I'm glad to see you safe and sound," Papa planted a soft kiss on her forehead. "C'mon, now. Let's get you to bed."

They crossed the hallway to Remedy's bedroom, which was much cooler than the rest of the house and free of the foul smell. Remedy changed into a comfortable nightgown, feeling much more at home inside the familiar comfort of her cotton bedcovers.

"What do you think Grandma is doing right now?"

Papa tenderly stroked the space between her eyebrows, for it always made her fall asleep. "I think that wherever she had decided to go, she is thinking of us."

Remedy could feel the smile in his voice. A wave of peace engulfed her at the idea that her grandmother was thinking of her. The gentle pressure on her forehead carried her to the edge of drifting to sleep, when she suddenly remembered. The view of the still ocean hit her at once, and she decided to put her trust into Papa. "Papa, you've never let me down."

Papa had always been there to explain, to understand, and to hold her through all the growing pains and lessons of life. Anything uncomfortable or difficult that arose, he would be there to guide her through it.

"You've always told me to trust my instincts, and I promise I wouldn't be saying this if I wasn't worried." She had now opened her eyes, sat upright, and leaned against the wooden bedframe.

"What is it, sweet child?" Papa looked worried, and although she didn't want to cause his worry, Remedy was glad to have his attention.

"Before Grandma …" She paused to gather her strength. "Before she died, she said death was not her choice. I feel it in my gut that something is wrong; her death was a violation of free will. She wasn't truly ready to depart from this world." It was a relief to get this off her chest.

"Remedy, but why didn't you say anything before?" Papa looked genuinely surprised and taken aback.

"But I did, Papa, and you took no notice!" She raised her voice without meaning to.

"I am so sorry, Remedy. I don't remember ever hearing this. Please tell me more," he said with eyes wide open, awake more than ever.

Remedy told him about Sacnicte's death, how fearful she had been to let go, and her warning not to trust something or someone.

"She also mentioned *him* coming back, or something."

Papa's face paled, and she realised that whoever her grandmother had in mind, Papa already knew.

"My love, did she say anything else, anything at all about *him*?" Papa tried to ask calmly, but Remedy could hear fear hiding behind his voice.

"No. She passed shortly after …" Remedy wished she had something more useful to say. "Papa, who is this *him*? Please tell me what's happening." She sounded alarmed and knew her instincts had been right all along.

Something was coming. An impending change was approaching. Yet despite Remedy knowing change was a way of evolution, regardless of whether it was good or bad, and that change was to be embraced in this moment, Remedy wished nothing had changed and her grandmother was still here. She had always known what to do, and Remedy needed her, perhaps more than ever.

"There's one more thing you need to know."

Papa stared at Remedy, eagerly waiting for her to say more.

"The water, the ocean, it has stopped moving, as though time itself has lost momentum," Remedy said slowly, as though keeping the truth in her mind would make it somehow less true.

Papa ran to the window with Remedy right behind him. Even with the help of the bright full moon, the dark ocean was impossible to see. Yet the silence of the night was all the truth they needed. The absence of roaring waves crashing against the rocks was almost painful to hear.

The moment felt like a surreal dream, one that you wanted to but could not wake up from. It was as though the outside world had ceased to exist and all the life Remedy knew was inside her bedroom.

"I must see this with my own eyes." Papa rushed across the bedroom. "If this is true, we have no time to waste."

"Wait for me at the front door."

Papa nodded and quickly closed the door behind him.

The next couple minutes passed in the blink of an eye. Filled with adrenaline, Remedy changed from her nightgown into warmer pants and a purple woolly jumper, which her grandmother had knitted for her. The hallway was dark, as the lifetime of the candle wall lights had expired. Remedy impatiently felt the wall for the artificial light switch to illuminate her way, only to give in and walk down the stairs in the dark. She stretched her arms alongside the width of the staircase, with one hand on the wall and the other on the glass banister.

"Papa," she whispered to the darkness as she stepped off the last step.

The room was dark and cold. The awful fire smell was stronger than before, as though the burning object was still in the room. Remedy scanned the space until she noticed a dim light coming from the table lamp next to the large swivel armchair.

"Papa?" she said quietly, approaching the light. Remedy stopped halfway across the room as soon as she spotted a pair of unfamiliar black ankle boots next to the legs of the chair. They looked tough, as though they had been through a lot, with some scuffing on the surface, yet the base looked durable and sturdy. Something felt uncanny about them; they seemed exceptionally and certainly unnecessarily thick skinned for the warm climate of the kingdom.

The chair slowly crept around, revealing the boots' owner. Papa was reclining in the armchair, smoking a thick cigar. He had changed into black satin trousers and a red shirt. The cigar smoke smelled like the colour yellow—not the warm yellow of sunlight and sunflowers or hay but a sickly yellow that sticks to the inside of your nostrils. It was eye watering, and she could taste the acrid taste on her tongue.

"Remi, whatever can I do for you?" he said with a smile that could not be trusted.

Remedy was lost for words and could not recognise the man who sat before her. "Papa, are you feeling all right?" she asked, despite already knowing the answer. Papa was not himself, and she had only seen this version of him once before, at the burial when he had been cold and agitated. He had been a stranger then as he was now.

"But why, of course. Are you feeling all right?" he said in a concerned, sarcastic tone.

Remedy chose to ignore the game he was playing, remembering what she had planned to do. "Papa, we must go now. You said it yourself; we have no time to waste." She heard the fear in her voice and knew Papa heard it too.

He inhaled the tar of the cigar into his throat and slowly blew the smoke into the room. The stale fumes travelled in the air, hitting Remedy's throat and making her cough as though they had momentarily set her lungs on fire.

"It's for the best that you go back to your room now." Papa's eyes were dull and his face unamused as he glared at Remedy standing frozen in front of him.

Her face was hot with fury, disappointed, and with the last fight left in her, she snapped, "You always told me that I could count on you! Today, you've lost my trust." Remedy donned an armour around her heart to help hold her emotions at bay, despite her feet feeling weak, as she waited for Papa to respond.

Instead, he slowly swivelled the chair away from her.

"Something is not right, and if you don't feel it, then I believe you have lost your way, and I shall seek guidance from the elders," she said with the knowledge of the weight that such accusations beared.

In the early years of childhood, everyone born into the family of the guardians was taught that even the brightest of souls lose their way; Remedy was no exception. She knew that although very unlikely and yet not entirely impossible, a soul could be misguided by both their own inner shadows and external forces. It would be then the duty of their loved ones to help the one who had lost their way walk back on the path of light. If Papa, the grand guardian of the kingdom, had lost his way, then the life and destiny of the whole kingdom was in danger.

"There is no need, Remi. Your father is just fine. I will investigate the water, but I must do so alone," he said in a deep and husky voice. It was the most masculine voice Remedy had ever heard, and she could not be fooled; this was not her papa's sweet and gentle voice. The papa who read her bedtime stories and sang her lullabies as he stroked her hair had a mellow voice of an angel.

Remedy knew this crooked voice and frantically searched her mind for its origin. Her heart pounded harder, slowly but loudly against her chest. It was the voice of the darkness she had heard in the forest.

She began to slowly retreat when the voice said, "No goodnight kiss for your papa?"

Remedy's jaw tightened at the thought of kissing the cigar-stained skin. "Papa, I wish to go to sleep. I am very tired now," she said courageously and continued to retreat towards the stairs.

She was glad the voice did not respond, and as soon as her feet touched the edge of the cool, marble stair, she turned onto her hands and knees and, like a frightened animal, ran up the stairs straight into her parents' room. The air, unlike downstairs, was fresh, and the windows were wide open. Mama's record had finished playing, and the needle kept tracking the dead wax on the vinyl, creating a low-level surface noise.

Remedy lifted the needle off the record player, closed the windows, and locked the door. She stood at her mama's side for a moment, watching her sleep peacefully, unaware of the unwanted guest in the room below. Careful not to wake her, Remedy slid between the sheets and closed her eyes.

That night, she dreamt of her feet sinking into tarlike sand, unable to run, and out of breath with smoke in her lungs. When she awoke, Mama was no longer next to her, and the room was as she had left it the night before: dark. Only the illuminating full moon shone through one of the windows, giving light on the wall clock that showed six minutes past six. The sun had not risen.

CHAPTER 14

THE LAND OF THE DEAD

The warm, golden sun penetrated through the thin layer of skin on Whalina's eyelids, forcing her eyes to open. Slowly becoming aware of the familiar surroundings, she was surprised to see Neal sitting beside her on the wooden bench. "Did you see her?" she immediately asked.

"See who?" Neal responded calmly, interlacing her fingers with his.

The brown river ahead flowed at the same smooth pace; everything seemed normal and untouched. Unsure how to proceed with the flow of the conversation, Whalina feared this was yet another episode from the *other* world.

"Do you remember when we were on the train coming back from my parents? The day I picked up my painting?"

"Of course, I even have pictures." Neal chuckled as he scrolled through the photo gallery on his phone and finally clicked on a picture of Whalina sleeping. "Sorry. I couldn't help myself. You slept until the very last stop," he said with an innocent smirk.

Whalina realised Sacnicte had never been real, not in the palpable, physical way that she was. The ghost had come from another plane and had wormed her way into Whalina's mind. She'd become a friend, someone trusted who had played a role and influenced her to step off the train of life that she had led in London. Sacnicte had told Whalina it was her duty to find a way back home, hinting that this was the missing ingredient she needed to feel whole, happy, and complete. The ancient wisdom of the old woman could not be denied; indeed, wholeness must be reaped from within, but the directions given had been ambiguous.

In the middle of the Amazon jungle, with visions and blackouts, Whalina felt far from belonging and more of an outcast than ever. Knowing Sacnicte had never been real, she was determined to see her again and seek the answers needed. With no way to conjure her presence, Whalina had only one other person in mind.

She found the shaman in a secluded part of the herb garden, where most herbs and plant medicines were grown. Some herbs were more known in society than others. Nettle or chamomile, for example, were common in Europe. But the mystical properties of those herbs were still not widely accepted. Only the dedicated and chosen ones could speak the language of nature and understand its language. The shaman's chosen disciples were allowed to enter the garden, but only Wind was permitted within the inner-fenced area. Hidden in its own private garden was a singular tree, no taller than six feet. Its leaves were coarsely toothed margined, rich in green and fine hairs.

Standing at the gate of the secured garden, Whalina did not want to intrude but couldn't help but watch the shaman work with the plants. Wind delicately picked the tree's offspring, beautiful white flowers with shades of light pink, and placed them inside a small straw basket. After several minutes, he removed his gloves and walked towards the entrance. A bright smile ran from his sun-strained eyes. He looked happy to see her, and Whalina instantly felt better.

"I was hoping we could talk," she said confidently but wondered whether Wind could feel her energy radiate with hesitation. The west wind whistled a sweet fragrance into the air, instantly bringing Whalina out of her head and into the now. "What is that smell?"

"It is the angel trumpet flower." He opened the basket.

Whalina gasped with shock, seeing that the angel trumpet was in the shape of a bell, the same which Sacnicte had held. "You grow this, *here*?" Her wide owl-like eyes appeared more prominent than usual, and Wind passively nodded in response.

"What is it that you wanted to talk about?" he asked and waited patiently as Whalina soaked up the silence.

Suddenly, it felt like coming here was fate, and no matter what path she would have taken, life would have always brought her here.

"I want to do the soul retrieval now," she said with a flawless execution of words, as though a weight had been lifted off her shoulders, bringing relief of finally arriving at the stop which would take her home.

Wind had been ready for this; after all, the flowers were for her. "I need to prepare the medicine. When the time is right, I will find you." He briefly placed his hand on Whalina's shoulder, sending an awakening current of goosebumps down her spine, then strutted away. The shaman had a distinctive way of walking, with his back immaculately straight, as though a puppeteer from above was in charge of his path.

"Wait for me!" Whalina shouted, running after him and quickly becoming aware of the decline of oxygen being carried to her lungs. Forced to slow down, she knew he would wait. "Tell me about this trumpet flower," she said out of breath.

Wind sat on the dry soil in the middle of the path.

Whalina followed his lead and sat in front, with the open straw basket between them.

"For eons, shamans have used the precious angel's trumpet in rituals and ceremonies." He gazed at the flower as he continued teaching Whalina how the ancient mother plant allowed shamans to communicate with their ancestors. Under the influence of the plant, their psychic visions strengthened, and they could travel across realms. The right preparation and quantities were needed for the communication between the spirit world and a human soul to occur. A gram less or more could create undesired effects, including death. Despite its seemingly angelic benevolence, the sinister plant was highly toxic. It had been the cause of a permanent crossover journey for hundreds of spirits. When ingested, powerful stimulants affected the central nervous system, causing hallucinations and delirium, which would then be followed by a coma. The medicine could also be applied externally, leading to acute paralysis of the sensory nerves. Only a skilled shaman was allowed to harvest and prepare the medicine.

"Whalina, you will ingest the plant," Wind whispered, slowly closing the basket.

"Sorry. Could you repeat that?" Whalina was sure she had misheard.

"You heard right, Whalina. The flowers are for you." Whalina could hear the compassion behind his voice. He knew she was afraid.

"But I'm not a shaman. I thought you would journey to the spirit world like the first time, and I will lie awake, waiting for you," she argued, followed by several shallow breaths.

"No one will save you, Whalina. The only chance you have at bringing your fragmented soul home is if you find it yourself. You must be your own saviour," he said unapologetically, for it was the truth that could set her free.

"You are exactly where you are meant to be. All those synchronicities have come together for you, bringing you here so you can fulfil your purpose."

Whalina knew she needed not to question the part she was about to play in the revival of her soul but to trust the process.

*****

The journey home would not be simple. Wind explained how the anticipated trip would begin and end. Yet both he and Whalina knew what happened in the spirit world could not be predicted. He drew a map showing their position in relation to the place that had been housing half of Whalina's soul for over two decades. The shaman used the metaphor of a tree to visually conceptualise the path she needed to take. The tree bark was life on Earth, its leaves were the upperworld, and the lower world was the roots.

Traditionally, the upperworld was the house of angels and peace. Some called it Heaven, whilst others believed it was the place where spirits rested and regrouped. Each living being on Earth had a soul, and once physical death occurred on Earth, the soul would travel to the upperworld to heal and meet with their spirit master. Together with a higher consciousness, they would initiate a soul agreement outlining the next steps they needed to take for their soul's evolution.

Wind explained everyone was born with a soul agreement, which held the soul's mission on Earth, as well as the lessons they needed to learn. Some spirits descended on Earth, needing to learn the act of forgiveness. Others wanted to master unconditional love; occasionally, all a soul wanted to do was heal past hurts. No soul agreement was the same, and the upperworld was always known as a place of retreat and sanctuary. Moss, Wind's grandfather, used to tell him bedtime stories of how serene and beautiful life after death was and that there was nothing to be feared.

However, when Wind travelled across realms to find Whalina's soul, he had a very different experience of the upperworld than what had been promised. Today, the upperworld held no resemblance to Heaven. The old place of sanctuary had been drowned in darkness, becoming a hostile, unstable environment. This was where the wildfire broke loose and swallowed Wind under. For an inexperienced traveller, such an experience could entrap the soul in fear and turmoil forever, making it impossible for Whalina to return. The upperworld had changed; something or someone had destroyed all that was good and had turned the promised land into a battlefield.

Whalina continued to be enticed with Wind's analogy as he explained the tree's roots were traditionally known as the Underworld or Hell. This was the path he wanted Whalina to take to reach the other realm that held her soul.

"You want me to go through Hell?" she gasped and ripped the fresh green grass from the soil.

"Yes, I need you to trust me. 'Hell' is safer than what I saw in the upperworld." Wind's voice was firm with determination; there was no room for negotiation. He explained that her idea of Hell was not what she had seen in movies or had read about in books. The lower world was a place where all human history was recorded and where, very often, wounded parts of a soul would flee to. When this happened, the human psyche would greatly suffer due to the debilitating gaps in their soul.

This was where Wind anticipated Whalina's fragmented soul had been residing after he had seen it was not on Earth, but, as he explained, it was not where he was guided to. The lower world was a maze of conflicting emotions and turmoil, which could follow one back into the middle world. Only skilled wayfarers dared to travel there, but the risk of getting lost was higher in the upperworld than in the roots of Hell. Whalina was to travel vertically down the axis, and then horizontally to the right, which would bring her out of the lower world and into the dimension where she had lost her soul.

Whalina noticed the damage she had caused to the grass and crossed her arms. "Will you go with me?"

"Although you may not see me, I will be by your side." Wind's voice remained firm, and Whalina wished he could soften and just tell her that it would all turn out well and that she would be okay.

"And if I get lost?" She wiped the sweat collecting in her palms on the grass.

"You will have an anchor, something that will keep you grounded and connected to Earth."

Whalina looked puzzled, and Wind explained that throughout the ceremony, her mind might wonder and that it was crucial for her to recognise when that happened. This was when the anchor would serve its purpose; Whalina would need to refocus on the purpose of the quest.

"When you begin to wonder about idle things and objects that may come your way, remember, you must find the whale and will your soul to reconnect with you."

Whalina nodded in agreement. "What is the worst thing that could happen to me?" She looked down to pick at the grass again.

"You will return empty-handed, just like me last time, and we will try again." His smile reassured Whalina that she would be fine.

Sometimes the truth could do more harm than good; in this case, if Whalina knew the truth, her fear might hinder the mission's outcome. Her life was good as dead if she did not follow through with the calling she was destined to fulfil.

*****

When the sun had set, Wind called everyone to gatherer under the kapok tree. The Aztec and Maya culture considered the tree to be sacred. They believed it was a symbol of the link between Heaven, Earth, and the world that was believed to exist below. It was here where the journey across realms would take place.

Whalina lay on a comfortable bed of blankets and watched the full moon in the cloudless sky. The wind made itself heard by interacting with the trees, and the enchanting sound of rustling leaves created a song with the crackling voice of the fire. If one focused closely enough, they could hear the passing river in the far distance, and all four elements—earth, water, air, and fire—were present.

Wind prepared the sacred space by using the smoke of the holy stick, also known as *palo santo*. The indigenous people of the Andes had used the natural wood for centuries as a spiritual remedy for purifying and cleansing energies. Wind believed the smoke would favourably aid her journey and ward off evil spirits and misfortune. Once the wood fragrance filled the space, Wind smudged himself and everyone involved in the ceremony. Each person represented one of the four directions.

Neal sat in front of a volcanic rock, acting as an agent for earth. He was always the one who grounded Whalina and was the person who made her feel most safe. Sarah wore a hat made from warrior bird feathers, such as the eagle; air was the symbol Whalina associated with her sister. Sarah reminded her of lightness, innocence, and courage. Wind had chosen Mikey to bring water into the ceremony; he was the guardian of the seashells Whalina had brought with her from Cornwall. Finally, Wind had tasked Icaro with playing the drum, but he was also the fire chief in charge of the fire needed for the ceremony to begin.

Wind smudged Whalina last and focused on the intention of clearing fear and hesitation. It was imperative that Whalina surrendered and entered the underworld with purpose and courage. Wind faced each cardinal direction in turn and called them into the ceremony, blessing and thanking them for their continued support of life on Earth. Wind continued the initiation process, whilst Whalina studied the moon shining directly on her. Her mind was empty. Before the ceremony, she had been worried that intruding thoughts would not let her relax. But she was calm, the same way she'd always felt in the water.

"Beloved ancestors, blessed you are, as I ask you to come forth and join us in the search of a lost soul. May you guide and keep her from harm's way, and so it is done," Wind announced humbly.

The fire gusted, and although she did not flinch, the scorching heat spread throughout her still body.

The shaman knelt by her side. "The time has come."

Whalina eyed the small cup Wind handed to her. At the bottom were a few drops of the angel trumpet medicine Wind had prepared. As per the instructions, Whalina whispered a prayer to the plant. "Thank you for coming into my life. I ask that you keep me safe and bring me back home." Then, in one gulp, she swallowed the most acidic juice, reminding Whalina of vomit. Grateful, she drank the glass of water Wind had handed to her and looked to him for guidance, asking with her eyes, *What's next?*

"Now, remember to surrender. Don't fight it."

With the shaman's voice repeating in her mind, Whalina lay on the ground and watched the moon shrink as her eyes closed. The shamanic drumming beat made every cell of her body vibrate and dance in unison. No thought could interfere with the penetrating beat that made her soul come alive. It was one of the most pleasurable moments in her short life on Earth. Feeling ecstasy without a shadow of fear or doubt, Whalina knew she was exactly where she not only needed but wanted to be.

Icaro's hands were hitting the bowl-shaped drum, and its sound vibrations paved a road to the lower world. Whalina felt warm and comfortable; her body was light, and it all felt too easy, too peaceful.

The drums ceased, ripping Whalina from her ecstasy and into the land of the dead.

CHAPTER 15

LIFE IN THE DARK

Time: The First Day That Belonged to the Dark
Location: The Fallen Kingdom of Light

Remedy ran downstairs and opened the front door. She stood barefoot on the cold floor, confused and filled with disbelief. "But how?" she whispered to herself. There was no logical explanation as to why the sun had not risen that morning. Life depended on the sun. Without it, every living being would cease to exist. The sun was a portal for the souls to travel into their next life. Without sun, the souls of loved ones would be stuck in the in-between without a body but pure floating consciousness in the land of the living.

Remedy thought of her grandmother.

"Mama, Mama!" she shouted and turned back to the house, running straight into Papa.

Inevitably, he put his arms around her. He carried the familiar fresh scent of geranium—the smell that Remedy had grown to love since she was a child—but to be sure, she searched his eyes. Papa had warm and welcoming eyes filled with radiance, like a campfire at night. Small wrinkles at the sides were owed to the gentle smile below. This was the Papa Remedy knew and loved.

"Papa?" Remedy hesitated to say more, uncertain of everything she thought she knew.

"Of course, dear. Who else?" He laughed nervously.

"Remedy love, we need to speak," Remedy heard Mama say.

When she peeked behind Papa, she saw a figure sitting at the dining table that had been a gift from Kai's father many years ago. Made from oak tree, durable and strong, it was made to last. As Remedy approached, she smelled the pot of hibiscus tea brewing on the table. The room was murky, with only a couple lights switched on in the kitchen, and Mama's face became clearer once Remedy sat at the table.

"How did you sleep?" Mama was making small talk, and for Remedy, it was a sure sign she, too, was nervous.

"The sun … is Grandma …?" Remedy couldn't find the words to ask whether Sacnicte's soul had transitioned into the afterlife as expected or whether she had been stranded with no way out of this world.

"We cannot be sure, but trust that she journeyed to the other world with the last sunset." Papa's voice was melancholy yet genuine; Remedy wanted to believe him. Unable to face his daughter, he stood with his back to her, and she could feel the high walls between them.

"Last night, we intended to see the frozen ocean together. When I came downstairs, you were different, cold, and said you must go alone." Remedy paused, needing to take a deep breath. "Papa, I have begun to wonder whether it is possible that something, someone is manipulating you." She eyed Mama, who was clearly forcing the faint smile.

Mama reached across the table and cupped Remedy's small hand into her own, as though covering Remedy's hand could keep her safe. To a stranger's eye, the small gesture might not seem much, but to Remedy, it was confirmation that Mama knew what Remedy had imagined.

"Around four in the morning, I woke up sitting in that chair." Papa pointed to the chair where the voice had sat the night before. His face looked fragile, as if he might crack and shatter into a thousand pieces.

"I thought you never came down, and I fell asleep waiting for you. You must believe me, Remedy. I then went to see the ocean myself, and every word you said was proven true. The ocean was sealed." Papa watched his jittery hands. "I am so sorry to let you both down."

The man who Remedy thought was all-powerful, invincible, and strong, her hero, was full of doubt and fear. The sight inspired a range of emotions in her: fear, frustration, and sadness, but the most prominent emotion was anger. A fire-like sensation festered in the pit of her stomach, urging her to move, to act and to fight. Whatever or whoever was the reason behind the disruption of peace, not only in her family but within the whole kingdom, had to be stopped, and there was no time to talk, not when lives were at stake.

"Papa, you haven't let anybody down, but we can't sit back and watch the world we know and love fall apart," Remedy said with confidence and purpose like never before; for the first time in her life, she believed her actions could make a difference. She could use her skills for the greater good.

"Until we know what we are up against, we need a safe word, something that will tell Mama and me that this is really you we are speaking with. Do you remember the necklace with the gemstone you gave me after I faced my fear and flew with Jupiter for the first time?"

"Of course, I do. You made me so proud that day."

"The next time I see you, I'll ask you what type of gemstone it was, and if you don't answer correctly …" Remedy couldn't bring herself to say what her gut was telling her to do. It was the duty of the guardians of the land to do whatever was needed to protect the kingdom, to preserve the light in people's hearts, to allow them to evolve without fear, and for their purpose and destiny to be fulfilled. Remedy knew what had to be done. If darkness consumed Papa's spirit, there was only one way out.

"I know, my darling. I accept and trust you to do what must be done." Papa stood from the table. "I am going to seek answers from the elders." Before Remedy had a chance to ask, Papa concluded, "The sea is unknown right now. It's too dangerous. I shall go alone."

The elders lived in the bodies of whales and spent most of their time in the ocean's deep waters. They were thought to be ancient gods who, by choice, incarnated in the light realm to guide people in their soul missions. They were considered soul masters and helped raise the realm's vibration. They were the descendants of the guardians of the land who had lived thousands of years ago when they, too, had the duty of protecting the land from darkness. In their whale reincarnation, their purpose was to protect those who travelled from home and to lead them back when the time was right.

When a soul decides to reincarnate into a new body, they come with a purpose. Still, sometimes that purpose becomes distorted during one's lifetime, so the elders help the soul find a way back to themselves and help them on their journey home. They may appear in dreams or influence life synchronicities to send humans a message in their waking life. They come to the surface of the water and offer guidance only when it is truly needed, and no one really knows how to summon their majestic presence. The magnificent power and wisdom behind the eyes of a whale penetrates deeply into a human soul. When one looks inside a whale's eye, their life will never be the same again.

Remedy had never met an elder whale, and she'd hoped there would never come a time when one would appear in front of her, for that would mean she had lost her way. "Papa, will you be all right?" Remedy couldn't help but wonder if perhaps she should be the one who sought help for her father.

"The whole kingdom is in chaos over the sun's failure to rise. Our people need you, Remedy." Mama rose to her feet, with her large belly prominently sticking out in front.

Remedy clenched her fists and tightened her jaw. Something was out there, threatening her vulnerable mama and playing mind games with her papa. The strong desire to protect them brewed inside her, and it was the only thing she could focus on.

As soon as Papa left for his exploration at sea, where he and his men would try to break the seal of the ocean, Remedy went outside and called for Jupiter. As though he could sense Remedy's agitation and was on standby, the great lion appeared right away at the palace door. Remedy quickly climbed on his back, and without a need for verbal communication, Jupiter ascended towards the moon.

It was half past eight in the morning, and the air was cooler than ever. The sun had been absent for over fourteen hours, and the atmosphere was missing its warm embrace. Remedy wore a long armour suit which reached her knees. It was made from a strong, durable fabric, created to keep the cold from penetrating their bones. The robust shell of the surface was impenetrable to wind or rain, and soft cotton lined the inside to keep the skin warm.

Remedy's hair furiously blew back as the kingdom had never experienced such powerful winds. Each gust felt like it could be Remedy's last as she clenched Jupiter's mane. She could just about keep her eyes open as they glided through the open sky. The full moon was bathing in its marvellous glory, as though a victory had been won; he finally owned the sky. The town square was busy and loud; inaudible mutter travelled skywards as Remedy hovered over the town for a safe space to land.

"Your Lightness, Remedy! Is this the end?" one man shouted from the ground, and row by row, people turned their heads skywards for answers. Men, women, and children frantically moved, paced, and searched for answers.

Whatever happened to trusting the process? Remedy thought. People gave into fear at the first sign of trouble. Their glow of light, usually so bright over their faces, was dim, and in one or two people, the light was on the edge of extinction. Remedy's own light was at risk as her heart and mind raced irrationally in opposite directions. Her mind argued that it was impossible to calm the herd.

They had reverted billions of years to their animalistic ways. Fights erupted over food supplies, they ripped unripen fruit from the trees, and those who knew how to listen could hear their high-pitched cries. Without the sun, there was no life. The whole ecosystem would collapse, and a new way of existence would take place, one where humans must fight for survival.

The intoxicating fear rose through the air so pungent that Remedy could smell it. A metallic, bitter, and unsettling fusion of sweat and tears made her heart swell with sadness and empathy for her people. She recognised so many of the faces below. There was the flower lady who tended to the most sublime lavender field and the young man with the round glasses who made the best lemon tarts in town. The family who looked after the wild horses, the Fowler's, were here, together with their twin daughters.

Remedy and Kai had spent weeks on their land when they were all children. They had observed the horses, given them names, and let their imaginations go wild as they talked about the unique personality of each one and the adventures they had.

Remedy decided to descend, confident that now was as good a time as any. Jupiter slowly landed in the centre of the small amphitheatre, and as people gathered around them, he spread his bird wings wide, forcing them to keep their distance. As Remedy stepped to the ground, she realised she had no idea what to say. She was a firm believer in always telling the truth. Nothing proved more honest than when one opened their heart and expressed their very essence to the core. Yet today the truth would only be the cause of more suffering.

Remedy decided it was best to keep the uncertainty and worry surrounding Sacnicte's death and Papa's unusual behaviour to herself. People were already scared enough, and it was her duty to inspire love and ignite light inside them.

"My loved ones, my warriors, and lightworkers, I am here to tell you the truth of what is happening to our beloved kingdom." Remedy's voice trembled, and as much as she wanted to present herself as confident and strong, she felt far from it. So many pairs of eyes fixated upon her, hungry for answers, desperate for hope. "Our kingdom is under attack." She watched faces turn from expectation to confusion. "Right now, my father is out in the sea, seeking guidance from the elders, and I am confident in the answers he will receive." She paused as people murmured between themselves.

"The ocean is sealed. How do you expect him to get across?" an elderly man asked.

A couple years ago, Mama had donated several books from the palace's private collection to the public library. Remedy remembered the man from that day. He was the one who had given a public speech and thanked Mama for her generosity. Remedy did not have an answer; she tried to focus her thoughts, but the crowd's whispers grew louder.

"The seal was broken this morning. I witnessed our guardian's departure," Kai said. He was standing in the top right corner of the amphitheatre, and unlike Remedy, he had a voice made of steel. It carried perfectly through the air, delivering a blanket of courage upon reaching Remedy.

She smiled inside, knowing she was never alone. Someone was always looking over her, whether she could see them with the naked eye or feel their warmth inside her heart. "I promise you that whatever is coming, we can fight it. But we can only do so if we stay united. We must keep our hearts open, let love flow in and out freely, and let the light stay shining within each and every one of you. Only then do we stand a chance with the darkness!" She looked for Kai, only to find a gap where he had been standing.

"Your Lightness, what about food supplies? When will the sun return?" a woman with a child at her hip asked.

In all honesty, Remedy had no way of knowing when the sun would rise again, but if she lied and were later proven wrong, she'd lose the people's trust and respect—something that took a lifetime to build. "I admit we don't know when the sun will rise." She paused, allowing people to digest the truth, and continued before they had the opportunity to open their mouths. "But I know that as long as we stay abundant, caring for one another, we will not lack, and all we need will be provided." Remedy closed her eyes and slowly hummed the vibration of the word yum.

The sound was believed to hold the power of entering the heart and sewing together any cracks and holes; that may have happened due to emotions of low frequency, such as anger, fear, or guilt. It was the sound of love, and love could heal anything. Like the domino effect, one by one, people took hold of each other's hand, closed their eyes, and hummed. They shut down any intruding thoughts as their energy imprinted to the present moment, where only union and love could exist.

Remedy saw that despite being in a state of fear, inspired by an innate instinct to survive, people hadn't lost hope and could still return to their prime state of existing in love. Remedy stayed with her people for many hours, humming peace into their existence, until a gentle touch on her arm took her out of the meditation. It was Kai.

He had blood up to his elbows, and tears streaked his face. The strong man who had carried her through the forest the night before appeared broken. She couldn't allow anyone to see him. A sight like this would inspire great panic. He was trying to tell her something, but the loud humming from the thousands of people in front of them made it impossible to hear. Remedy took her armour suit and covered Kai's bloody arm.

"Remain present and await my return," she addressed the crowd in a loud, clear voice.

The kingdom remained still as Remedy and Kai mounted Jupiter and flew towards the red coast.

Chapter 16

The Gate of Hell

An uncanny fog, lazily floating through the empty, fruitless land, guarded the underworld entrance. The visibility was zero to none, and even a small candle flame would go a long way. Through the thick mist, Whalina drew her hand close to her face to check that her body was still intact. Pale more than ever but at least physically present, the petite hand found her long hair tangled with thorny ice. The white air filled the gaps between the skinny fingers as her hands carefully waved around the circumference of her body. After finding no obstacle within the small surrounding perimeter, it was time to step forward into the unknown.

The ground was raw and earthy. It was moist as though a long monsoon had just passed. Whalina's bare feet melted into the soil as she took the first step with both hands extended in front and expected to hit an invisible object. Her chest was heavy with anticipation as she slowly ran her hand through the thick mist and found what could be an icy stone at the edge of her fingertips. Her heart raced as the frost stuck to her skin, and she recoiled. Walking alongside the stone wall, not knowing where the path led, she was learning to trust the unknown, the unpredictable. She was letting go of control.

With her right hand touching the wall and her left scanning the air, she anxiously stepped onto the dirty snow. Its white purity was tainted with dark spots, as though someone had taken a bucket of black paint, sprinkled a small yet significant amount, and turned the once perfect snow into something grey and damaged. The encompassing silence created an echo of every step taken, making the crack of a twig sound like a broken bone. Whalina's mind gravitated to Neal and their first Christmas together. On the morning of Christmas Day, Neal had awoken her with a small splash of snow, which immediately instigated one of the best snow fights of all time. The whole of London had been snowed in, and they had run outside barefoot in their pyjamas.

Whalina looked down and realised the fog had marginally reduced. She could somewhat decipher the shape of her feet and the washed-out blue colour of her dress. The fabric reached just below her knees, and the long sleeves covered her arms. She wondered who had dressed her and why they had not thought to give her shoes when the stone wall came to an end, and her hand reached a gate. On the other side, beyond the iron bars, was a mirror reflecting her own image, making it impossible to see through. Whalina looked inside the hazel eyes and felt the pain of her severed soul. For decades, she had felt a void inside, an ache to connect, to be more than she was capable of being.

"Hello? Anybody here?" Her throat was tight, as though an iceberg was forming inside her mouth. Whalina looked up to see the tall gate reaching beyond the mist. If there was a Heaven, the height of the gate would surely reach its doors.

Occupied with the grand measures of the gate to the underworld, she shrieked when she noticed a tree vine had intertwined with the outer bars of the gate and wrapped itself around her wrists. The slimy green branches appeared endless as it moved fast down the gate, and the more Whalina fought to get free, the tighter its grip became. The excess of the thorny vine compiled and tangled around her feet, making it impossible to move. Blood trickled down her arms, staining the blue dress and the white snow.

The cunning branch squeezed whatever life remained and Whalina gasped for air, then, at last, the vine loosened its grip and fell lifeless to the ground. The slime began to drain away, and the thorns retreated inside its stems. Whalina knelt to inspect the leftover broken branches and found them to pulse in a breath-like motion rising up and down every three or four seconds.

Losing her balance, she fell backwards onto the ground and watched the vine rise from its deathbed. Drawing at no more than six feet high, arms and legs extended to take the shape of a man. The bright green faded, and an olive-coloured skin came through. Still on the ground, Whalina watched in awe as pieces of fabric flew and collected from all directions, forming a long cloak with a beautifully embroidered pattern of green, red, and blue. With the sound of the being's loud sigh, the fog cleared, revealing an elderly man with dark plaited hair. The wrinkled hand reached for Whalina. Surprising her with his strength, he pulled her up to stand. Whalina wanted to introduce herself, but her lips would not obey. It was as though the ice had sealed her throat shut. The elder had a gentle look about him, and it was hard to believe that just seconds before, he or the vine he was created from had been wrapped around Whalina's body.

"I am Amara. I am the gatekeeper of the lower world. What is it that you are seeking here?" Amara's lips curved into a smirk, and Whalina's voice returned at once.

"I need to enter the underworld and find the lost half of my soul." She looked straight at the gate as though its metal chains could break with her gaze. She avoided eye contact with the elder's golden-green eyes, knowing little about his principles.

Amara's cold, long fingers grabbed Whalina's shoulders, pulled her onto her toes, and froze her body in place. His fingernails pierced her skin, and when their eyes finally met, Amara had the introduction he needed. At once, he released her shoulders, and Whalina dropped onto her feet. It was Amara who was lost for words now; the chosen one had finally arrived, and this was how he had greeted her.

Focusing on his naked feet, he remorsefully said,

"Please forgive my behaviour, Princess." Whalina stood at a distance from the elder. Confused by the change of tone and afraid he might again change his mind, Whalina decided to take advantage of his sudden kindness. Conscious of time running out, she needed to get through the gate and knew the princess could do so. "Amara, I need you to open the gate."

"Of course, My Highness. I shall open the gate at once. Pardon my idiocy." The elder bowed to Whalina, and with a gentle wave, the ice surrounding the gate melted, and the mirror behind broke. Its shattered pieces scattered through the air, leaving no trace, and the metal gate burst open.

Whalina stepped forward and stood at the open entrance of the underworld. The road ahead was empty and, in the distance, split into three different paths.

"Amara, what I'm looking for is not here. I wish to travel across dimensions. Is there a map I could use?" Whalina asked, playing the part that Amara had assigned her.

"Why of course, Princess. I have been waiting for centuries for your return. The underworld is, how does one say it nicely ... *overpopulated*, and it is very easy to get lost. With the destruction that happened above, every soul is dumped here without a way to move forward." Amara paused and sighed. He was deeply saddened. "Anyhow, I will no longer waste your precious time. Your route is quite simple, and the map will guide you. May I, My Highness?" He proffered his hand.

Whalina hesitated before reaching her hand to the gatekeeper. She thought Amara was reading her palm, but his eyes had closed.

"Whenever you're ready, Princess."

Whalina panicked. She had no idea what the old man meant, nor what would happen if she told him that she was no princess but an ordinary girl with a life on Earth. "Amara, it's been a while. Please remind me," she whispered.

"Of course, you've led a human life until now. Close your eyes, open your heart, and tell your soul where you wish to go."

The cloaked man's eyes remained closed, and Whalina felt inclined to close hers too. Inside, her thoughts ran wild in tune with her racing heartbeat. Searching for the answer, which should come naturally, Whalina was puzzled with amnesia. Something was lost and needed to be found, or maybe she was lost and needed to find a way back home—home to Neal and Sarah.

The strong wind blustered, shaking her into place. Home to Wind—Wind, the shaman, of course. The longer she stayed here, the less clear her human memories would become. Wind had foreseen and warned that this could happen but had promised the anchor would stop her from wandering too far. She pictured an anchor at the bottom of the sea and an image of a whale, the large body swimming freely through the ocean waters and inside the piece of her that she needed back.

"The map is ready, Your Highness." Amara stepped backwards, allowing Whalina to look inside her palm.

A road map with a sky-blue flashing light was imprinted inside her palm, leading to the destination marked with a small anchor symbol. "Thank you, Amara. I will now be on my way." Whalina closed her palm and nodded goodbye to the gatekeeper.

"Be safe, and remember, you are never alone. Your ancestors are walking beside you." Hearing Amara's last words, she crossed the gate and entered the lower world.

Silence filled the air, and Whalina was relieved and hoped it would stay this way. She glanced back and saw the gate had vanished; there was no going back. Time was the enemy, and with every second she was not walking forward, she was taking a step deeper into the ground of the underworld. Wind had made it clear that getting out of the underworld with only half a soul intact was impossible; the only way out was through.

Whalina opened her palm and saw that the map was zoomed in to her current location, with the three roads ahead. With every step, she noticed the surrounding world took shape. Trees that were at first transparent turned solid, and the sky was no longer misty white but dark with heavy clouds. The once identical three paths revealed their own stories as each one took a unique form. Ice covered the road to the left, perfect for an ice-skating rink with welcoming hot springs ahead. Steam overflowed from holes in the earth, inviting Whalina to relax in their hot, soothing waters. Studying the map, she saw dull, lifeless grey marked the left path, and miniature fire-spitting volcanoes filled the path on the right. However, the middle road flashed blue.

Without hesitation, Whalina approached the green forest and into a horrific smell. She couldn't place the scent, but it reminded her of the time when she had left uncooked chicken out of the fridge. The smell churned her stomach, and she felt herself beginning to gag. Quickening her pace on the narrow but clearly cut path ahead, she was determined to get out.

Tall trees edged the path, and Whalina found it difficult to see past their first line. It was as though the forest was an illusion, something someone had created for her eyes to see. Perhaps if she strayed off the path and ventured deeper between the trees, she'd walk into nothing but darkness. Recalling her anchor, Whalina marched ahead towards the sound of distant thunder.

Amara had said the underworld was overpopulated, but not a living—or dead soul, for that matter—had yet crossed her path. Apart from a low-groaning hum, the forest was silent, which made her wonder whether the gatekeeper was telling the truth. Perhaps the dead were invisible, or maybe she was invisible to them, like a ghost usually would be on Earth. In either case, Whalina was positive she was alone.

She regretted not asking Wind or Amara how long this journey would take. Time was an ambiguous concept in the underworld. It seemed she had only just arrived, but the waxing crescent moon straight across was racing and quickly becoming quarter full in front of her eyes; yet not a single sunrise had come. Her bare feet were tired and had minor cuts, but there was no time to rest; the thunder was becoming louder. Whalina managed to peek at the map inside her hand and knew she was coming close to a second turning point.

At last, the blinding flash of the lightning brought the dark forest into light, illuminating the source of the groaning hum and what lay behind the front row of trees. Deeper in the forest, all trees had human heads instead of branches. Women, men, and children of all ages were dead but somewhat alive. Maggots resided inside eye sockets, hair patches were stuck together with dried blood and rotting flesh, and worst of all was the mouths which hummed the tune of death. Those souls were most in pain, clinging onto hope, knowing no redemption remained in this world. They were new, and their humanness had not yet left.

Such is the nature of humans, to hold onto dead things—things that no longer serve them in any way, things they deep down know they need to relinquish but cannot. Attachment is one of the greatest sources of pain, a yearning to hold onto something forever, but in the end, we are all left with nothing but our soul.

Whalina sprinted through the black forest. The ground was muddy and difficult to see, and she had no time to check the map. She tripped over fallen branches but continued forward with the gusting wind running beside her. All this time, she walked side by side with the dead, and if it wasn't for the thunder, she'd still be unaware. The importance of being conscious and aware, doing everything with total presence, was highlighted. What the eyes could not see, the mind struggled to understand.

As Whalina ran, she did not look back; she was fixated on the full moon ahead and unaware of the pouring rain that had drenched her. Inhaling the pungent smell of decay made her nauseated, and when she finally stopped running, Whalina fell to the ground, out of breath. Her back was pressed against the wet, soft mud, and the sleeves of the once blue dress was ripped beyond repair. With the moon hidden behind clouds, the sky was black, and not even a single star was looking out for her soul. Whalina screamed at the top of her lungs and heard the wretched sound echo back.

"Where are you?" she whispered through a mouthful of tears, remembering Amara and his promise of the ancestors being with her. Black-and-white photographs of her grandparents who had died before she was born came to mind. She tried to remember their names, but her lips could only say one name: "Wind."

The air was hot and humid. Even he had abandoned her. Warm tears stained her rosy cheeks, and she looked to the dark sky and closed her eyes.

*****

When Whalina was a child, she was terribly afraid of the dark. As well as illuminating the hallway, Teresa always left her daughter's bedroom light on. One evening, soon after the birth of Sarah, Whalina announced that she would no longer fear the dark but, instead, would be brave for her little sister, and from that night onwards, apart from the small, plastic stars on the ceiling above her bed, all the lights were switched off.

*****

Disoriented and confused by her whereabouts, Whalina jumped to her feet. The sky was still inky black without a trace of light, apart from a lone star that had appeared in the far west. Her eyes lit up with hope that, after all, someone was with her. Although it was just one star, that was all it took for the path ahead to become clearer. Sometimes, all someone needed was for one person to believe in them, and soon their belief and love would light the way forward.

Following the map inside her palm, Whalina headed towards the western star. With the absence of grass and trees, the road was arid, as though land and water never met. The path was lifeless, with no colour or sound, making Whalina feel like a character in an old black-and-white western. Any minute now, a black mustang could come by, and if it did, without hesitation, she would jump on top and gallop until she found the sunrise—the feeling of wind blowing so hard that you could not hear or see clearly, let alone think about anything else but the present.

Black mane hair would lick her face, leaving a gentle sting, making her sharp, alert, and feeling every movement of the strong, robust muscles as they bunched and released, the feeling of becoming one with your horse and trusting fully that he can take care of you. Whalina had never ridden a horse before but knew the feeling well and could almost relive it right there and now.

Puzzled at how much knowledge and experience surfaced about horses, she recalled Amara calling her a princess. Under normal circumstances, she would dismiss and laugh at the idea of previous lifetimes, believing everyone was given only one life, and when that was over, it was over. But nothing about her was normal. Her heart was beating back on Earth, whilst her soul and consciousness were walking through Hell. The gatekeeper of the underworld had called her a princess, and she couldn't prove him neither right nor wrong. Perhaps if there was such a thing as past lives, she might have been a princess.

Far in the distance, Whalina thought she could see small specks of light. Excited at the idea of finally finding the sun, she fiercely ran downhill, unaware that below the ground was the lake of fire, and the temperature of the soil beneath her feet was gradually increasing. The air was oppressively heavy; pressure built inside her chest, and the specks of light were coming into focus. Fire. For every two wildfires roaring with rage, two more were behind, burning greater than the ones that came before. It was like a never-ending burning country field. The fire was hungry. It was eager and waiting to massacre anyone who dared to come through.

Whalina stood at the entrance to the abyss of Hell. Sweat dripped from her forehead, and her lungs begged for air, chocking with smoke. But the map inside her opened palm had led here and was urging her to continue. Overwhelmed by the heat attacking from all directions, she retreated.

"Whalina!" someone called from inside the Gehenna.

For a moment that seemed to feel like an eternity, Whalina stood motionless. She had to focus, and all became silent. *Sarah.* The decision that followed was automatic, as though she was conditioned to always protect her sister, and just like that night when Sarah had called her crying, Whalina had no choice but to run right into the entrance of the devil's mouth. Nothing could have prepared her for this, but somehow, she was ready.

The soles of her feet burnt as she jumped from leg to leg, navigating through the fire jungle. Fortunately, the blue dress was no longer knee high and was barely covering her body, allowing her to move swiftly in and out of the dancing fires.

"I'm right here." Sarah's voice became louder, and Whalina knew she was close.

Expecting to find her sister trapped inside a circle of fire, her gaze froze on Neal.

Naked, he stood at the edge of the spitting black tar lake. His once pale skin was burnt, covered with thick blisters and cracks, almost unrecognisable to the man she had fallen in love with. Being pushed with a wooden stick, he was centimetres from drowning in fire. The demon penetrating the wounded skin had its back to her, but judging from the thick brown hair, Whalina was sure it was a woman.

"Neal, I'm coming! Hold on!" She ran towards him. Miscalculating the size of a fireball, she jumped and fell onto a sizzling rock. Adrenaline pumped through the heat-swollen veins, and without noticing that her forearm had been cut to the bone, Whalina pushed on towards the demon.

"I'm begging you, please stop!" Hot air carried Sarah's cries, and as Whalina turned around, she saw her little sister suspended from the wrists. Sarah's feet were tied with a stone pulling down the weight of her body, ripping tissue and muscle, whilst their mother carved into her skin with a cat o' nine tails whip made of leather, ivory, and rope. The whip moved fast like a razor, slicing into the skin and releasing blood through the laceration.

It suddenly hit Whalina that all her life, she had been a bystander to the injustice and double standards of her mother. She had stood on the side lines, watching their mother treat and love Sarah differently. Whalina felt her guilt surface. All these years, she had lacked the courage to face Teresa head-on and make a stand for the family scapegoat. At last, she could finally make things right.

"I pray, don't do this," Neal pleaded with the demon, who briefly turned her head. It was Whalina—or, at least, someone who looked exactly like her. She was the beast thrusting the stick into Neal, pushing him closer to the edge.

Whalina felt her heart rupture into a thousand pieces; the two people she loved the most were on the verge of dying, and she only had time to save one. It was an impossible decision to make; they both needed her, and she would have to turn her back on one of them. Standing between the two, she closed her eyes and blocked the surrounding sounds of burning fire and screaming.

"Go forward." Wind's voice circulated around her aura.

Whalina looked up and watched the fire disperse to the sides, creating a clearing ahead. Some kind of opening appeared at the end of the path, but for Whalina to see what it was, she would have to get farther from Sarah and Neal. *My anchor.* Whalina took a deep breath, and everything around her stopped. The enraged fires were suspended mid-air. Whalina surveyed the mass destruction. Even if she tried to save Neal, he could no longer be saved from falling into the vicious, scalding tar. Whilst Sarah's screams had been silenced, her head bowed to the ground, and a pool of blood had formed below.

Whalina exhaled the breath she had been holding, returning to the chaos. She had to choose between her beloved sister and the love of her life. The overwhelming shame and guilt of failing at being their saviour crushed her heart, but she had to save herself. Without looking back, she ran down the momentarily empty path ahead, leading to a staircase. Whalina ran up the spiralling twists of the cold stone stairs. Eventually, her lungs could not keep up, and she was forced to slow down and look at the map.

The lines inside her opened palm were white, and for the first time, a flashing red light signalled the last turn to the left. Ignoring the Saharan thirst in her throat, Whalina pushed forward, checking the map, until she had reached the small red dot. Slowly walking between the two walls of the narrow stairs, Whalina searched for the final turn that would lead to the other dimension and noticed a blue door.

Looking closely, she saw pressed white flower petals, in the shape of the number one, decorated the doorframe. Despite the sticky black tar that seeped from under it, the closed door was the most beautiful thing Whalina had seen in the underworld. The door creaked as she slowly opened it, revealing the most daring of all cliff edges. There was no land to step on, only a grey sky and a few irrelevant clouds. Holding tightly to the inside of the underworld walls, Whalina leapt forward, finding the entrance to the other world was right in the middle of the ocean.

Facing the clouds, Whalina found it impossible to hear the ocean whispers hundreds of miles above sea level. The only sound was the blasting wind. Whalina leapt back and firmly shut the door. Her heart pounded at the thought of jumping into the unknown, but she had no other choice. *I did not get this far only to get* this *far*. She knew the only way forward was through the door. She had to *trust*.

With a leap of faith that this was the place where Amara, Wind, and all her spirit guides had guided her to, Whalina opened the door. She spread her arms like the most powerful of predators in the sky and fell through the air. Diving into the dark, blue sea, she let go of fear and set herself free.

CHAPTER 17

THE PURPOSE

Time: 1 Hour Before Remedy Makes Her Choice
Location: The Fallen Land of the Kingdom of Light

From the height of the sky, Remedy saw the ocean had once again been awakened. The waters were boundless, screaming with freedom, able to finally roam without limitation. The ocean seal was broken, and it appeared that Papa had succeeded at returning balance, at least to the waters. Yet something still did not feel right. The sea was furious, as though it was at war with itself. Remedy had never seen such tremendous waves, and they only seemed to be getting bigger and more outraged.

Kai squeezed Remedy's waist as he sat behind her on Jupiter, signalling that it was time to descend. He jumped off moments before the lion landed on the sand and ran alongside the coast. Remedy kissed Jupiter on his big, cold nose. Something inside told her it would be a while before she would see him again, so she wrapped her arms around the big animal for a moment longer, then ran after Kai.

The sand was soft, and it felt like her feet were being pulled under, making every step a little harder to get up from. Out of breath, she finally saw Kai up close. He was no longer running but stood frozen in front of the roaring storm. As Remedy approached Kai, she became paralysed with shock. Unable to move, her breath was involuntarily suspended, and for a moment, she thought she might never breathe again. Surrounded by red water, an elder whale had been washed up on the shore. Remedy frantically scanned his body, finding that his eyes were closed, and he was not breathing. The girl finally inhaled, and as her lungs expanded with air, the smell of the rotting flesh filled her senses.

A small part of her died. She lost a small segment of hope, like losing a battle she didn't know she was fighting, and the question of who the opponent was still remained unanswered; that was when the worst of all thoughts came to mind.

"Kai," she whispered, as though their presence had to remain a secret. "Whose blood is on your clothes?" She remained fixated on one spot of the whale's body: the head where the harpoon had pierced the flesh. "Kai, I need you to answer me right now."

If Kai had anything to do with the elder's death, it would be her responsibility to ensure he never harmed another being again. Kai was her best friend, and although they had never said 'I love you,' she had loved him since the day they'd met. Punishing Kai and sentencing him to imprisonment for the rest of his life would be the hardest thing she'd ever had to do. Still, for the kingdom, she'd do anything.

"I didn't do it, Remedy." Kai regained his voice, and a weight lifted off Remedy's chest.

She faced him and saw the sadness in his eyes. He was just as confused and afraid as her. One of the bravest men in her life, who had carried and kissed her with a river of passion hours ago, was broken.

"I saw him washed up on shore. I tried to close the wound, but I got here too late," he said with deep pain in his voice.

Remedy had reason not to believe him, and many unanswered questions circled her mind, yet her gut told her that Kai was telling the truth. She had never caught him lying before and, deep down, couldn't believe he would ever harm another being. Kai had a good soul; the glow around his face had not diminished, and he was of pure heart. Remedy found herself again immobilised with panic as the reality of what was happening sunk in.

Grandma was gone. Mama and the unborn babe needed her protection whilst Papa was out at sea, lost in ways more than the physical. Remedy felt more alone than ever; there was no guidance or set of instructions on what to do next, yet everything she did or didn't do could have lasting effects on the kingdom. Suddenly, the realisation that the fate of the world was in her hands had arrived. Only yesterday, she was a carefree child, whining to her grandmother that she wanted to have purpose and make a difference in the world. Today, she was a woman, aged overnight, with the potential to fix the world or to stand by and watch it deteriorate. Her intuition was hinting at a theory, which if it were true meant her world would never be the same again.

"*Remedy, Remedy,*" she heard someone calling her name, bringing her out of the deep waters of her thoughts and into the now.

"Remedy, your father is approaching," Kai said quickly and stepped aside as Papa came closer.

"A moment with my daughter," he ordered in a clear authoritarian voice.

Kai politely nodded and slowly retreated farther back.

Remedy turned around and saw that he did not go far and still had his eyes on her.

Papa's pupils were so dilated that little white was left in them. His clothes were drenched, and his bouncy curls were stuck to his forehead. "What you see in front of you is an act of deadly sin, and justice will be served to the one responsible for this," he spoke fluently, as though his words had been rehearsed, and pulled his hair back into a sleek ponytail—something Papa had never done before, for he always let his hair free.

"Did you speak to the elders?" she asked, suspicious of his uncharacteristic hairstyle.

He raised his eyebrows, his face lacking empathy. "I would have if someone had not put a harpoon through the elder's brain," he answered sarcastically, pinching his lips tightly together.

Remedy studied him for a sign that would give *him* away and hugged her arms around herself. "Did you see anyone else at sea?"

"Are you insinuating I had anything to do with this?" Papa put his fingers on his forehead while shaking his head.

"No, that's not what I—"

"You should question the boy. He was first at the crime scene." Papa pointed at Kai, who stood several metres away but surely could still hear his stern voice.

A new train of thought formed in Remedy's mind. Papa could not be sure that Kai had been the first to find the whale unless he had been here first, observing from a distance. It seemed he knew more than he was willing to share. Remedy took a deep breath and exhaled through the cold air. There was no way she could reason with him. The more Papa spoke, the less she believed his words.

"Will you be going to sea again, Papa?"

"Well, someone ought to do something. Otherwise, we'll soon be known as the Kingdom of Dark," he said and turned towards the marina.

"Papa!" Remedy shouted out of desperation. *It's now or never.* "Here, you gave this to me when I was brave. May it give you courage." She handed him a hollow wooden pendant in the shape of a circle, on a thin white rope necklace.

Papa eyed the piece of jewellery presented in the small hand and smiled.

"I gave it to you for a reason. Keep it." He walked away with his back hunched over and his heavy feet kicking the wet sand.

Remedy stood motionless. Her body had shut down, yet her heart was hammering. Blood rushed through her veins, her ears rang, and her mind went into overload. Thoughts, feelings all mixed. The pressure inside her head was at its peak. It was as though several ropes had been tied repeatedly, creating a brain full of impossible knots.

"Kai ..." She had finally found her voice. "I need to get on that boat with him."

His warm hand caressed and held her wet, cold shoulders. "Remedy, please tell me what I can do to help."

With a huge sigh, she turned towards him and hid her face against his large chest. She wanted this moment to never end, for she knew that as soon as she told him the truth, nothing would ever be the same. Unable to dam her heavy tears any longer, Whalina closed her eyes and allowed them to escape and streak her face.

"That was not my father. His body has been compromised, and I need to take out whatever is inside him."

"But ... how?"

"I made the necklace for my little sister for when she is born. Papa had never seen it before. I was suspicious, but now I am sure." She had regained her strength and found a new stream of courage.

"I need to speak to the elders before he kills again." She broke away from Kai's embrace.

"Remedy, you, out of all people, know what this means," he said, slowly looking straight into her eyes.

"I am not going to kill my father. I believe there's still a chance. I just need guidance from the elders. Kai, this is my purpose. I must save the kingdom." And for the first time, she truly believed every word she said.

CHAPTER 18

THE LAST LIGHT

Whalina had never seen the majestic face of a whale up close before. Once, in Seaworld, she had watched a show, but never again after learning the horrific conditions the sea animals were kept in. It was like limiting a human being to a small, square room, when a whole world was out there to explore. To say the whale was big was an understatement. She was surprised at how human the eyes of the sea mammal seemed. The same way one can read a person, what they were feeling, and whether they were likely to harm you or not, Whalina detected the whale was calm and just as curious about her as she was about him. With a wealth of knowledge behind its eyes, the giant was trying to tell the story of how her soul had entered its body.

Whalina noticed a bright light radiating from her skin, illuminating the whale's beautiful iridescent blue skin. She also realised she had been breathing under water without holding her breath. Moving her hands across her neck did not lead to a pair of gills. In fact, she was breathing normally through the nostrils. She recalled the night of the accident; she had always been able to breathe under water. The logical brain and imprinted social conditioning had taught her that it was impossible, that human lungs could not breathe under water, that we as a species were bound to walk on land. If Whalina had known she could breathe under water, the possibilities would have been endless; she would never leave the sea. From a young age, she had been cautioned about her limitations and only in a matter of life and death could the animalistic instinct override the limiting belief.

That night of the lake accident, Neal had seen her 'die.' Whalina had stopped fighting and moving. Neal's body had begun to shut down, and in the split seconds between water entering his lungs and him beginning to drown, Whalina had been able to breathe under water and got them out. She had never been in any real danger.

The magnificent creature observed Whalina in awe. She was just as extraordinary to him as he was to her.

Whalina looked into his innocent, bright eyes and saw her own reflection, not the banal mirror image that she saw in the bathroom mirror. The deep-blue eyes explained that she and the mammal were one. Whalina saw her fragility and vulnerability inside the largest animal in the world. She was the whale, and the whale was her. Feeling the rush of blood in her ears, neither was afraid as Whalina moved closer. They had known each other intimately before, and Whalina felt the excitement of coming home as she reached to touch the divine face. The most powerful animal in the realm intended to remind her where she had come from and who she was.

The whale parted his lips slightly, and when Whalina willingly swam inside his mouth, all became dark, and suddenly, she stood by the window frame of a beautiful but unknown room. The windows were glassless, allowing warm, floral air to flow freely between the patterned ceramic walls. Each square had a different pattern, painted in a unique arrangement of purple flowers; no square was the same, and they all existed indifferent to each other. Below the window was a picturesque field with many different species and colours of flowers, most of which Whalina could not name. Trees scraped the sky, and several white horses rested under their shade, only they had horns between their eyes. The sky was baby pink, or maybe midnight blue. It seemed to change colour with the direction and strength of the wind, unable to be captured.

The chamber was as big as Whalina's entire apartment, and in the middle was a large four-poster bed made from old rustic oak, covered with bed sheets white as snow, contrasting the rainbow-coloured leaves that hung from the top of the frame. At the end of the room was an easel made of nothing else but pure gold and behind a girl with a singular plait that just about touched the white marble floor.

Whalina inched towards the girl, curious to see the picture, when a woman entered the room—Sacnicte. The four walls appeared brighter in her reflection as she approached the canvas girl. The elder woman was dressed in a long, light-pink dress with eyes bluer than the ocean waters, Whalina could not take her gaze off the blinding beauty and elegance. The girl was not at all bothered by the radiant being who stood and watched her paint.

"How many hours have you dedicated?" Sacnicte's voice was as delicate and soft as Whalina had remembered.

"One hundred and eleven days." An ounce of sadness resided in the girl's voice.

"Patience, my love, your soul purpose will be revealed in due time." Sacnicte stroked her hands through the girl's soft cottonlike hair.

"I know, Grandma. I just wish I could be of use already."

Whalina was curious to see her face, but the girl's focus remained on the painting.

"Sweet child, have you noticed any peculiar behaviour in your papa recently?" The question made Sacnicte lose the smile in her eyes.

"No, Grandma. Why do you ask?"

Unsure why, Whalina felt deeply saddened for the girl. Empathising with their cause, whatever it could be, she felt anxiety rise in her body as the room turned silent and she could no longer hear their conversation. The girl got up from her easel, finally showing her face. With a sense of familiarity, Whalina couldn't shake the feeling she was looking at herself. The girl, of course, looked different, had hair several shades lighter than her, and could also be taller, yet something inside her reflected Whalina's own self—not in the traditional way of an identical image but more that she could be identical on the inside.

The girl and her grandmother left the room, and, at last, the painting was revealed. It was Whalina's *Soulless Woman* painting, her passion and nightmare art piece since she had been a young girl. This version of the painting was also not finished, and the space in the middle of the figure's chest had been left empty. Suddenly, it all became clear. All the puzzle pieces Whalina had been collecting finally came together. She could make sense and understand all that had been happening to her. She and the girl were one.

Whalina ran after them, opened the grand chamber's door, and stepped onto a boat. Standing beside the princess, she observed Papa and his men talk quietly, pointing to the horizon, then to the grey map on the table. All the men had long hair blowing in the wind. Only Papa's thick curls were neatly tucked into a ponytail. He was muscular, strong, and utterly fearless; Whalina remembered how she always thought of her papa as invincible. He knew the answers to all her questions. He was her best friend and hero.

The boat rocked on the unsettled waters, and the furious waves crashed into the boat's sides. The princess held onto the tall metal pillar, hiding behind its width, with only her large pearl-shaped eyes on display.

An enormous whale leapt freely from the water, revealing its powerful body. Papa grabbed his harpoon, closed one eye, and took aim. The princess screamed and ran between the whale and the weapon, but Papa was invincible, after all, and never missed his aim. The harpoon pierced the delicate skin on the girl's chest, hooked her beating heart on its sharp edge, and forever lost it in the ocean.

"Remedy!" Papa screamed and ran to his only daughter.

Warm blood spread over the wooden deck as Papa's golden girl dropped to the deck and would never rise again. Papa fell to his knees, and the whole kingdom heard his cry. It was not only Remedy who had lost her light that day. Whalina watched the whale's life be spared and the creature return to the ocean. What no one else saw, that destiny-altering day, was the tall shadow standing behind Papa. Whalina saw the shadow darken as Papa's tears stained his face. The deeper the grief and sorrow the old man felt, holding his dead daughter in his arms, the taller and more defined the shadow became.

Two sharp, bull-like horns emerged from the top of the cloaked figure. At the base of the horns were deep eye sockets which slowly dripped with black tar over its facial bone structure. A long, sharp hook pointing down protruded from the middle of the skeleton's face where a nose would be. The hook connected another hook which would usually be the base of the chin. Three crooked fingers emerged from under the cloak and caught Papa's tears as they dripped off his face. The demon wiped the tears onto his own face, breaking the connection between the bottom and upper hooks, cracking the seal between the lips. A dense black smoke poured from the crooked mouth and engulfed the deck.

Whalina stepped from behind the pillar and ran to Papa. She knelt beside him, choking on her tears. "I'm so sorry, Papa, I let you down.

The whole kingdom depended on me, and I let everyone down." Whalina searched for the right words inside her burning with pain heart.

"I promise to fix this. I will make you proud. I promise to come back."

Papa would never kill an innocent, let alone aim for a whale, the realm's most majestic and powerful of creatures. In fact, the first and only recorded murder in history, when the soul did not voluntarily decide to part from the body, had occurred fifty years ago. They had placed a young boy named Tarquin inside an iron cage and lowered him to the bottom of the ocean, left to drown, after they had found him conspiring with dark spirits outside the realm, planning to open the Ecnesba Well. The well was nature's way of ensuring balance in the world, a place where an absence of light and lots of darkness could live. The well was hidden at the bottom of the lake, located in the king's garden of Ava. The royal family guarded the significance and importance of the lake and passed the information from generation to generation. Legend had it that the one who opened the well would have power over the upper and lower worlds, as well as the Kingdom of Light. The dark power inside the well was immense. Opening the well would mean colossal damage to the kingdom. The evolved human consciousness would become polluted by low vibrations of hate, greed, and lust for all things outside of oneself.

*****

Tarquin was an orphan, abandoned on a cold winter morning outside the royal castle. The queen quickly fell in love with the little babe's black-as-coal eyes, and the royal couple adopted him. Shortly after, the queen became pregnant with the first royal child. Naturally, the royal prince was next in the succession line, overlooking his adopted brother Tarquin. One night, Tarquin overheard the king speaking with his son about the Ecnesba Well; jealousy and spite festered in the young boy. From that night onwards, Tarquin became obsessed with finding the well and practised the forbidden black magic, which always required the sacrifice of an innocent.

One night, the king woke from a terrible nightmare and went for a walk in the gardens, where he found Tarquin in a deep trance, sitting around a wildfire with a young, beaten child whose hands and feet were tied. Although the child survived, he was never the same. Tarquin's execution was the very next morning. The queen pleaded all she could with her husband, but it was up to the royals to oversee that the realm never swayed to the dark side. The king could not afford the risk, so he sentenced his son to death.

Tarquin was placed under water for precisely sixty minutes, but when the iron cage emerged from the seabed, it was empty. The iron bars were unaltered, but Tarquin's body had disappeared. No one could explain what had happened or prove that Tarquin was, in fact, dead. It was decided that the secret of the Ecnesba Well and its power would die along with Tarquin and was never passed on to future generations.

Remedy had grown up with no knowledge of the Ecnesba Well. She had no idea that Papa ever had a brother nor that her grandmother had lost a son.

*****

Whalina stood helpless as the black smoke consumed the boat and turned the young men's blood into a thick, boiling tar that ruptured their organs and melted their skin from the inside. Liquid oozed from their pores, noses, and ears until nothing remained but a puddle of charcoal-coloured slime.

Papa stood frozen at the feet of his dead child and watched his most loyal friends fall dead to the ground. Remedy's body greyed, and with every gust of cold wind, it crumbled into ash. Papa was consumed with grief and despair; his weakened body stood no chance, and his mind could not defend itself.

"Missed me, brother?" Tar's voice was hard as a stone, and Whalina could feel his cruel laughter bounce off her chest.

Papa's tears turned black. He was made immobile, allowing his brother to step forward, taking full ownership of Papa's body.

Whalina opened her mouth and tried to scream, but her voice was muted. The world fell silent, the same way it did when under water. It was just the beating heart and the infinite water embracing her every move. Whalina's body felt light, as though her bones had melted and her muscles had gone to sleep. It was time to move on.

Whalina remembered who she truly was and how in her life as Remedy, the Princess of the Kingdom of Light, she had sacrificed her life for that of another, dying a traumatic and unexpected death. Without fulfilling her purpose in the given lifetime, she could not ascend into higher realms, and even if she could, Tar was on his way to destroy both Heaven and Hell. Her very essence was fragmented between two bodies in two separate worlds.

The half that longed to save her father and her kingdom from Tar jumped to the nearest source of life: a baby whale being birthed at the bottom of the ocean, bringing Remedy amongst the most powerful of gods. The other half of her soul fled as far as possible. Tar's presence threatened the existence of all in the Kingdom of Light, now that Papa's body had become his host; there was no telling what would happen next. As a method of preservation, the other half of the soul descended to Earth, hoping to one day return with the stolen light.

CHAPTER 19

REMEMBER TO COME HOME

NEAL

Neal was trying his best to stay seated and represent one of the four directions. The fire was no longer pleasant, and the oppressing heat was too much to bear. Although no one dared to say it, they all wondered how much longer Whalina could take. It had been over three hours since her soul departed on the quest of finding its missing half. Since then, Icaro had changed the rhythm and volume of the beating drums several times, adjusting to the tune of Whalina's beating heart.

Neal sensed something was not right when the slow hum of the drum accelerated and turned into a race. Icaro's hands moved faster than eyes could follow, and Neal could no longer stay still. He eyed Sarah, then Mikey, who sat crisscross with eyes firmly closed. Sweat ran down their faces. It was only Wind who appeared unconcerned by the heat.

He sang in a foreign tongue as he had done ever since Whalina's soul left her body. Some songs were in Spanish, others were what Neal thought was the language of the indigenous people. The shaman was perfectly composed, as though he, too, was in a trance with Whalina.

His sweet girl lay perfectly still in the middle of the closed circle. The horrifying thought that perhaps she may have died in the middle of all the noise and heat crossed his mind. After all, how could anybody know whether her heart was still beating? Neal could not take his eyes off the still body. She looked so calm and at peace. Surely, if something were wrong, Wind would bring her back and stop the ceremony, Neal reassured himself. Unlike the shaman, Whalina was not immune to the fire, and sweat trickled down her face and hands and to the earth beneath.

Neal noticed Whalina was digging her nails into the soil. Not in the gentle, natural way they would fall if she were sleeping. The knuckles of her left hand were bent at a ninety-degree angle; she was gripping onto the soil, holding on as though something was pulling her off the ground. A single tear burst through her closed eyes, and several others followed, streaking her face when mixed with the sweat.

Neal looked to Wind, alarmed and angry that only he was paying attention to his sweetheart. Forgetting everything Wind had said about maintaining the sacred circle throughout the ceremony and under no circumstance interfering with Whalina's process, Neal's instincts took over as he leapt forward and touched Whalina's hand. His entire past life flashed before him—his mother's green eyes and the candy floss feel of her skin; the pain of falling off his horse for the first time and the way his father's beard tickled him when they embraced; the anger when he found his mother had abandoned him for her own soul's purpose and his vow to always be the one in charge of his destiny; the taste of fresh spring water after running through the endless field; the first time he saw her face; the sweet sound of birds calling for their mother; the goosebumps on his skin when he saw her painting; the feeling of warm rain after three hot months in the sun; the smell of jasmine trees, the smell of home; lying on a bed of straw under the hot sun with the girl he loved to the moon and back, beyond known galaxies and stars; the way he could fly with butterflies inside his stomach when her lips met his; the illuminating smile that radiated with purity and love.

She had a fire inside her like no other. She was the definition of courage, and anything she put her mind to, she could do. She was the best thing about him. Her name was Remedy, and he would die for her.

*****

Neal's touch returned Whalina to Earth, and her eyes grew wider than ever before, penetrating his physical eyes, seeing right through him. She remembered their summers together, carving wood and riding horses, the way his long hair would blow in the wind as he waited at the top of the hill for her, the midnight swims around the golden coast and barefoot walks in the forest, their first and last kiss on the frozen ocean. His name was Kai, and he had always been her soulmate, in that life and the lives that had come before. This time, he had followed her to Earth with the promise to her mother that he would find Remedy and bring her home.

"Kai, you found me," Whalina whispered. They held each other for the longest time, enjoying the sweet moment whilst knowing it would soon come to pass. Whalina's mind was an empty vessel, and her physical senses were shut down. The mind was silenced, and the heart danced with joy.

"It's time to go home, Remedy, my love." He studied her beautiful face, seeing the woman he had loved for centuries.

WHALINA

Whalina wiped the tears from his face. It all made sense. Everything she had ever done, everyone she had met, all the places she had been, and all she felt had led to this moment. Indeed, she had never belonged in this world, and her soul's purpose was to return home. It was time, and she was ready.

"Will you come with me?" she asked.

"Always," he said with a forced smile. They were all trying to be strong, despite not fully understanding all that would happen.

"Wind, how much time do I have left?" Whalina asked with a sense of urgency.

Wind bowed his head in response. She understood.

"Sarah, Mikey, please come closer." She looked at the terrified face of her little sister. Inside, her heart was shaking out of her chest, knowing she would have to let her go. Kneeling in front of one another, Whalina took Sarah's hands into hers.

"I want you to live every day like it's your last. Love like you can never be hurt. Dream as though your life is eternal, because it is."

"I don't understand." Sarah's voice broke as she tightened the grip on Whalina's hands.

"I have to go, but my spirit will live on, inside you. We will see the world together; I will be with you through every storm and sunrise. You will grow old, and I'll be waiting for you on the other side. I'll make it beautiful for you. I'll grow a field of sunflowers, and we'll dance till the morning." Whalina burst into tears and wrapped her arms tightly around her sister.

All the adventures they had planned, memories yet to be made, those, too, would die along with her. Together, they cried as their hearts bled for what seemed to be no more but a moment, and in the end, that was all life was: a series of moments. It was not the duration of a moment that defined it. It was the moment itself and who one shared it with. A moment like this would be one Sarah would cherish forever. She'd be able to relive the last time her sister's heart beat against her own. She would try but wouldn't be able to forget how Mikey and Icaro had taken her into the house and how she had cried herself to sleep for a year afterwards.

"Whalina, you're losing light. You must go now," Wind quietly whispered, and Icaro understood his brother without needing words.

Whalina kissed her sister's forehead and watched Mikey take her away.

"There is no other way," Wind whispered.

Before the ceremony began, Wind had warned Whalina that she might not return. The best-case scenario was that her broken soul would reunite and return to Earth as one. The worst case would be her soul reuniting and staying in the other realm, meaning Whalina wouldn't wake up. After seeing Papa die, her soul began to fuse with the other half that was stuck inside the whale. If it were not for Neal, the two halves would have completely merged and Whalina would've never returned.

"Ali, are you sure you want to go back there? Winning the battle with Tar won't be easy," Neal asked, but they both knew Whalina had made up her mind.

"They are my people. He killed Papa with cold hands. He destroyed the upper realm. There is no Heaven after we die, Neal. Every soul is sent into purgatory. I'm the lucky glitch who can fix this." As she spoke, fire burnt inside her hazel eyes. "How do we do this?" She looked to the shaman for answers.

Wind opened his palm, revealing a small glass bottle.

"It will be instant. Find the whale, become one soul, and when you die, don't go towards the light." Wind's voice was firm with urgency.

"Walk backwards. You will have a chance to reincarnate in the dark realm. Whalina"—he looked straight into her eyes—"you will have to remember; that is your only chance at beating Tar. He doesn't know you're coming. You have one shot at this."

Whalina swallowed the saliva that had pooled inside her mouth. "And Neal?" She panned from Neal and back to the shaman.

"I will be right behind you, baby. We'll do it together," he answered before Wind could say otherwise.

"Thank you for everything, Wind." She took the bottle from his hands.

"It has been my duty, Remedy." The shaman smiled before closing his eyes and sang quietly whilst softly hitting the drum.

Whalina kissed Neal's lips, knowing it would be decades before they would kiss again.

"Forever and always." She held his hand and took one last look at his face. The dying fire cast a shadow onto his face; she tried to imprint each detail into her mind. He was the most beautiful thing she'd ever seen.

"I will find you," were the last words she heard him say before putting the bottle to her lips. Neal guided her head onto his knees and wrapped his hand around hers. Whalina fought hard to keep her eyes open for a moment longer. The sky split between night and day as sunrise bled into the horizon. It was wonderful purple shade, with a few clouds drizzled here and there, creating a lookalike lavender field. Drawing her last breath, she thought of floating in the sea, the salty water holding her body on the eternal ocean. She was going home.

PART 3

CHAPTER 20

THE COMPLETED CANVAS

Time: Fifty Years of the Darkness Reign
Location: Kingdom of Dark

The full moon shone brightly on the girl's face as she lay under her favourite oak tree. The moon was a symbol of hope, giving faith to people and encouraging them to believe the times when the sun ruled the days were not over. In another universe, it was still shining brightly, giving life to elsewhere. It still rose every morning and illuminated their moon. They had not seen the sun for over five decades, yet as long as the moon remained illuminated, so would the idea that not all was lost.

The girl had never seen the sun, for when she was born in the woods one especially cold winter day, eighteen years ago, the sun had already been exiled. Born under the starless sky, the girl had grown up listening to the older generation tell stories of the sun and how, once upon a time, it had loved to rise every morning. They would describe its warmth, said it felt kind on their faces and had the power of blessing pale skin with a darker tone. They would say it was like a glowing fire in the sky that gave life and energy to all creatures of the land and brought joy to anyone who bathed in its light.

The girl wanted to believe the stories, and every night before falling asleep, she daydreamed that one day she would see the sun with her own eyes. Some people had allowed themselves to forget, or perhaps it was easier that way, whereas those who had never seen the sun before had doubts—doubts that ran deeper than the deepest of rivers.

All they knew was the dark; all they ever saw was dark. They had learnt to live in cold, harsh conditions, and their hearts had hardened and closed. Yet, against all odds and the challenging cards life had dealt her, somehow the girl's eyes shone bright.

From the moment she was born, life had been testing. By miracle, a woman who could not have children of her own had found the girl in the woods one December evening, crying loudly inside a hollow tree truck. The childless woman had taken the child to the village, named her Eva, and watched the babe grow to the tender age of four. Misery followed Eva, as her adopted mother died from an illness, orphaning Eva once more. Little Eva had been passed from house to house, never having a home or family to call her own, until she turned fourteen and ventured back into the forest.

Eva had always been a wild child who belonged to nature, and so to the woods she returned. It was not the abundant forest she had read about in books but the closest place she could call home. The forest was far from thriving, but the ruler's black magic was enough to sustain a very basic, depleted form of life. The King of Darkness kept the realm barely alive, mixing whatever light was leftover with his own dark magic to fuel nature and whoever he allowed to live. Some thought him to be kind, whereas others called this form of life torture and would rather die than live under his rule.

There was no longer an abundance of fruit trees and vegetable gardens. The trees fought underground wars due to the scarcity of water, and whatever fresh produce grew often died before it could ripen. Yet somehow, people adapted and life continued. For the first time, people turned to the slaughter of whatever animal still roamed the land, be it goats, camels, or even domesticated cats. Greed, fear, and hunger festered inside their hearts, and the teachings of the Kingdom of Light were few and scattered across the land. Whatever light remained was not found in the hearts of the common people, and Tarquin would kill those who resisted his leadership, or they'd be lost in hiding.

Some said they lived in the caves of the far north, others that they ran underground operations; no one knew nor searched for the truth. Whoever was found conspiring against the King of the Dark was publicly executed, and Tarquin himself consumed their soul. This only gave him more power, for those souls still had some light and hope inside. It was a losing game, and whoever believed otherwise was considered a fool.

Eva was one of the handful of people who still had light in her, although she would never let it shine in public. One of the families who had taken her in during her younger years, the Duffy family, had warned her against being joyful in public. They had taught her to contain her light inside herself and only let her eyes shine bright when she was alone. The Duffys neither supported nor resisted the King of the Dark. They did whatever they had to do to survive. The family's elder, who still held onto her light memories, ensured that morale and light were kept alive.

Madeline was eighty-nine and fought hard for her family to keep faith that the saviour would come and bring back the light. Eva believed Madeline and thought of her as the closest thing she had to family. Every month, she would go to the village and visit her. She would often bring red berries that could be found only at the far end of the forest, and in return, they would share a cooked meal. They lived a modest and frugal life but managed to feed their family of four and have a roof over their heads.

It was the last Sunday of the month, and as the moon rose, Eva returned to the village that had raised her. The girl did not know fear. After all, she had nothing to lose. Dressed in the black and white fur she had inherited from a dead Siberian wolf, she strutted down the path that had been long ingrained in her mind. The Duffys were neither happy nor unhappy to see her, but Madeline always welcomed her with open arms.

"I have something for you." Madeline closed the front door and whispered in Eva's ear as they embraced.

Her wrinkly face was filled with light, so Eva allowed her light to show too. The light could flow and be exchanged, allowing them to experience each other's love and warmth. The light had a liquid feel, like a slow pour of syrup. Eva treasured such exchanges of light; it made her feel less alone in the world. It made her feel human.

The sweet smell of baked bread and cooked peas filled the house, and as always, dinner was served by the small fire. Eva sat on the wooden floor between Madeline and her granddaughter Raven; Maria, Madeline's daughter, sat opposite Eva. Maria's husband, Albus, had left two months ago in search of cattle, and a space was left in the small circle next to Maria, as though he could walk through the door at any moment.

Eva salivated as they held hands, and Madeline led a prayer of gratitude to the Light gods for the food they were about to consume. Mealtime was sacred, so they ate in near-total silence, cherishing each bite and chewing delicately, making the small portion last as long as possible. Eva was used to eating once a day, sometimes every other day in the forest, but she never had the luxury of eating bread, so such a meal was a real treat. She was used to finding dead animals who, themselves, had died of hunger and thus could avoid killing animals by the mercy of her own hands. She survived by trusting the natural cycle of life to provide for her, and when it was her time to go, she hoped to have an animal eat her too.

Eva knew the best spots to find red berries and green cabbage or the occasional potato. Yet eating with other people and having someone make a meal for her had a different taste, one which she could not replicate in the forest by herself. Even if the dining experience lasted no more than five minutes, it was worth walking fifteen kilometres to experience Madeline's warmth and food.

Once everyone had swallowed their last, precious bite, Maria and Raven disappeared to the kitchen.

"Do you know what day it is tomorrow?" Madeline was quick to ask.

Eva thought for a moment, even though she knew no answer would come. She had stopped paying attention to the days of the week and only counted thirty nights between her visits with the Duffys.

"It's your birthday," Madeline answered.

"It is?" Eva said, genuinely surprisedly, her big blue eyes shining brightly.

The old woman's trembling fingers handed her a box wrapped in a thin, transparent white paper. Eva was ready to unwrap the gift when Madeline stopped her and said, "Not today. Tomorrow."

Maria re-entered the room with her apron off, and Eva knew it was time to go. Leaving the warm, firelit hut and having the ghastly wind push her back into the forest felt somewhat more melancholy than Eva expected. Just because she was used to walking the path alone did not mean it was an easy path. In fact, the longer she was alone, the harder it became.

Eva longed to be a part of something bigger than herself, to belong and do something that would make a difference to the kingdom. She had searched for the rumoured light workers for four years and had travelled to the far edges of the forest but had never met anyone who would shine their light back at her. Only the moon would shine and light the way home to her hollow tree.

She quickly wiped a cluster of tears that had escaped and rolled down her fair-skinned face. So what if it was her birthday tomorrow? It didn't mean anything, just another year of living in poverty, struggling for survival; another year with only twelve evenings shared with Madeline; three hundred and fifty-three days of solitude; another year of a slow death for the people of the land, for a life without light is no life at all. What was the point of having light if you could not share it with others?

Eva's head spun as dark thoughts intruded her tired mind. They often came, especially in the winter, when there was little to eat and the temperature dropped below zero. Eva did her best to push them away, to find something she was grateful for or looking forward to instead. She thought of Madeline and the warm bread, her oak tree, and the mysterious gift she tightly held under her arm.

Unseen animals moved to her left and right, creating a soft and comforting noise of breaking snow. The forest ground was laid with a carpet of fresh snowfall. Its highly reflective white crystals bounced beams of light from the moon, scattering a little brightness in all directions, making the path ahead a bit lighter than usual.

Eva took comfort in hearing the creaking sound of the snow breaking under her feet. She felt more alive, knowing she was leaving a mark on a previously untouched, clear path of snow, knowing if someone were to take this path, they would know someone was here. Physically seeing her mark on the road helped her believe she was not just consciousness but a physical body that could move and change matter. Sometimes, when Eva spent weeks alone in the dark woods, she would wonder whether she was truly alive and awake or whether the world was simply a figment of her imagination or a dream. Although she was completely free, she was also completely alone. Walking on the snow and hearing her footsteps brought a sense of peace and made the journey pass quicker.

After several hours of walking, Eva finally reached home. The oak tree was faithfully waiting, the grey clouds had swallowed the moon, and the sky looked darker than before. Eva finally lay in the oak's hollow, where the air smelt slightly musky yet brisk and fresh to breathe. As Eva balanced between the land of the living and dreamland, the smell conjured feelings of nostalgia associated with a change of seasons or perhaps a new beginning. The sudden influx of this new energy and the hope of something better coming soon brought a small smile to Eva's face as she surrendered into dreamland.

There had been a time in her life when sleeping was all she wanted to do. The oak tree was her day and night. Every other human necessity blurred into the background. It was shortly after when she had left the village empty-handed and learnt what life alone truly meant. It was then when she had considered surrendering her light and travelling south. Like the others, she would be put to work, searching for the mystical moissanite stone.

Rumours said the stone had disappeared from the palace around the time when the Dark Lord had seized the kingdom. For centuries before, the elders had used the stone, composed from a fallen star, to travel across the realm for benevolent reasons or sometimes to simply carry a message or bring a miracle to a troubled soul in another realm. Today, men, women, and children of all ages dedicated their lives to either mining through caves, digging through fields, or diving to the depths of the dark sea in search of the one thing that would allow Tarquin to teleport with ease. The King of Darkness vowed to give an endless supply of food and shelter to the one who would bring him the stone. And so, people dedicated their lives in hope for a better future for themselves, knowing if they found the stone, the Dark Lord would bring another realm to destruction. No stone would go unturned until he had the stone that would allow him to travel to Earth and infuse humans with dark thoughts and dreams. He would turn their joy and love into darkness and hate.

If Eva did, in fact, break and decide to go south, she'd live out her days with shelter and food, breaking her bones and working for his evil cause. There would be no choices and thus no freedom, a curse and a blessing in one. Today, she thanked the gods that they had held her back and she had stayed put through the hard times, for although life was not perfect, at least her life was her own, and she lived it by her own rules.

She would sleep whenever she was tired and would search for food when her belly rumbled. In the spring, when the temperature would rise by a few degrees, she would care for the birds that fell from their mother's nests and helped the wandering fox or rabbit find their way home. Eva had always remained soft and humble. No matter how much the dark tried to harden her, she always found her way back to the light. Whilst Eva slept, the moon started another cycle, and what would usually be considered night-time, five decades ago was now the new day, for this was the only time when any light could touch the land.

Eva was extremely sensitive to the light, and as soon as the moon began to rise, her eyes opened. She enjoyed the brief moment of not knowing who and where she was. That precious moment, when the brain had not had its first thought of the day, was extremely short-lived and most elusive. Too quickly, Eva remembered her name. Her eyes wandered left, where the night winds had blown away the transparent wrapping paper, and a small, crumbling wooden box remained. Like never before, she excitedly jumped from her hollow tree and reached for the box. It was secured with a golden thread across it.

Eva took the shiny thread and placed it inside the hollow, knowing she would find a use for it later. Inside the box was a small notebook with just four white pages and a black and a yellow pencil. The paper had a thick, vintage-like feel; it was in no way fragile, and its white was of pearl colour. On the first page was note, written in the most beautiful handwriting, *When I was eighteen, a very wise, sage woman had given this to me, in the hope that I would find my purpose. I hope this will help you too. Love and Light, Madeline.*

A strong wind blew Eva's hair back, and the note sent shivers down her spine. Something was familiar about the words Madeline had chosen, something intimate that Eva's soul had recognized. She vaguely remembered drawing with her adopted mother before she had died, and she had not held a pencil for over fifteen years. It felt relatively odd in her right hand, and when she tried the left, it felt somewhat better. The pencil touched the pearl canvas of the paper and stopped, because Eva did not know what to draw. The moon was in its highest position, so if she were to draw something today, now was a perfect time.

The wind stopped howling, and just like that, everything was still, as though the whole universe had conspired to make this moment happen the way it did. Eva wanted to put the paper back in the box, tie the golden thread around it, and leave it for another time, but as soon as she took the pencil off the paper, the wind growled at her. Eva had read books about the four elements and how if one paid attention, they would notice the earth, water, air, and fire guiding them throughout life. It would often happen in subtle ways, and one would need to be open and observant to receive such guidance. The element of air called for the breath of life, a matter of life and death, and a chance at new beginnings.

As soon as she returned the pencil to the paper, the wind stopped. Eva closed her eyes. Trying to ignore her shaking hands, she did her best to calm her scattered thoughts. Her heart was telling her that this was important, that this was what she had been asking for all along. Still, doubt and mistrust filled her head, not allowing her to continue. She was and never would be special. She was an outcast and a loner, and the wind was just unusually temperamental today. There was no guidance from the elements. The books were nothing short of fantasy; real life is survival, gathering food, and finding shelter. It's about protection and survival of the fittest. There was no room for creativity in that equation, no room for expression or innocence, yet her heart was beating courageously, calling for a change and asking her not to give up on the pencil.

"Just this once," she whispered to her heart. The paper was essentially an empty canvas, ready to be transformed into something entirely new, something of meaning. She pressed the pencil to the paper with force, resulting in a large dark dot. Eva had forgotten that little effort was necessary to make a mark on the paper.

Once her hand loosened its grip, she slowly found rhythm. The pencil brushing was gentle and fluid, almost as though it had been rehearsed. To an outside spectator, it would appear that the artist knew exactly what she was doing. Her heart and hand formed an unbreakable connection, and it was all encapsulating for Eva who could not break away from the paper. She retraced some lines multiple times, as though highlighting their importance, whereas other lines were just about visible. The subject of her drawing was slowly taking shape.

The depicted woman in the drawing held her long wavy hair with her right hand so it would not drag on the sand. She wore no clothes; instead, her hair was wrapped around her wide childbearing hips. She was strong, not because of the defined muscles on her arms and thighs but because of the yellow light shining from her chest. Her eyes were fixed on the observer so that no matter what angle one would observe the picture, it always seemed she was looking back at the viewer. The woman's focus was incredible. She could tell a thousand stories with her kind yet daring eyes.

Eva stopped the pencil and surveyed the drawing. Something was not right; something was missing.

A green leaf fell from the sky and landed on the page.

"How?" she whispered to herself.

The trees were dying. The leaves were brown; the brightly green leaf had survived against all odds. Eva pressed the leaf onto the white paper, allowing its natural green fluorescence to come through and immaculately mixing with the yellow on the paper. Eva's heart beat hard and loud as she reached inside her pocket and found a lone red berry; she must have forgotten it when she had given the berries to the Duffys the night before. She hesitated over the pungent bloody red, as it posed the risk of being too strong and too bold, dimming the yellow and green colours from the woman's chest.

With a slow exhalation, Eva lightly spilled the red juice onto her right hand, and with her left index finger, she finished the drawing. The three colours shining from her heart reinforced the woman's power. Eva could see the sun in the yellow rays. It was warm and energising, yet also spoke of caution in getting too close to the sun and taking life in moderation and balance. The green reminded Eva of nature and how it fed her soul. Without nature, there was no life, no growth, and no matter how wealthy one was, without nature, life could not prevail; nature must always be nurtured and respected.

Eva understood why she had been uncertain of the red. It had the potential to be dangerous, to turn into blood. Its passion and strength could be transformed into anger and destruction under the wrong desires. Yet all three colours were needed for freedom. For if the woman's soul was white, she would not have any other choice but to receive and give light. It was the combination of the dark and light forces inside her that allowed for the choice of being kind and unkind. If humans only had light forces inside them, they would not be human, but instead, they would be pure divinity.

The meaning of life is not to be perfect; it is to be yourself—the light and the dark. Once the soul learns all its lessons, it will naturally be pure light and thus no longer human.

Eva understood that it was the dark that allowed for light to exist. In a world of pure light, there would be no colour, no vision, no shadow. There would be no growth or expansion, for if the world was entirely enlightened, there would be no space for more light. Everyone would be perfect and content by themselves and wouldn't need anything from anyone.

Eva studied the drawing, and her heart fluttered with excitement. The woman was familiar as though Eva personally knew her. Seeing the woman stand so mighty and powerful with the centre of her chest filled with the combination of yellow, green, red, and a dash of black felt to Eva as though she had found something she did not know she had lost. For the first time, light and dark had come together.

Eva's hands shook uncontrollably, losing the pencils to the snow and interrupting her moment of bliss. She tried to get to her feet, but the download of information, memories, images, and feelings flooding her mind overwhelmed her, and she fell into the cushion of snow. The world spun in front of her ocean-blue eyes. She thought she could see the sun behind the white moon, for it seemed to be shining brighter than ever before. The girl felt immune to the freezing snow beneath her as she relived the many sunrises and sunsets of her past lives.

The sound of the ocean and its most majestic of creatures rang loudly in her ears, sounds she had never heard in this lifetime, for the sea was in the south, and she had never visited the south. Memories of people she had not met yet she knew ignited a fire in the pit of her stomach. She smelled roses, followed by the sight of a girl with mousy brown hair. Eva did not know her name but knew the girl was important, then came the boy, the one who held her hand and who promised to follow her wherever she may go.

"Neal," Eva whispered as a single tear ran down from each eye and fell into the snow. The lifetime of memories rushed into her body, all the good and the bad—the journey of repeatedly creating the painting; the love she had experienced from the two people who had brought her into that lifetime; her dear parents; swimming in the open waters; the joy on the faces of the people she had loved the most; the heartache of finding out that she had to leave it all behind.

Eva lay on the crushed snow, unable to move, and just as she thought it was the end, her temples stung, as though a wild fire had been resurrected inside her brain. A second wave of memories, feelings, and traumas rushed in, and with no choice, Eva was forced to watch another lifetime of love and loss be given and taken from her.

Sacnicte. The name rang like a bell in her mind. The kind and fearless face of the woman she loved so much, Sacnicte gave her signs; if only she knew then what she knew now. The same forest and very same tree that had been her home for the last eighteen years was the exact spot where Papa and her used to rest during their horseback voyages. The rainbow colours of the streets filled with vegetables, fruit, plants, and flowers she could never remember the name of, the wonder of flying on Jupiter's back, whilst overlooking the Kingdom of Light, and the final day of her life happened so fast that Eva could do nothing but watch the unfolding.

The pain and despair of rewatching all that had gone wrong without a way of making it right wrecked her psyche. The harpoon pierced her heart, and just like that, the kingdom had fallen apart. Papa held her in his arms, until all that remained was the empty vessel of his only daughter's body.

Eva's heart beat hard against her chest as Papa's voice called her name one last time, "Remedy."

Chapter 21

The Weapon of the Heart

The world as Eva knew it had collapsed and with it, her identity. The two most important moments of life are the one where one is born and when one finds out why. Eva had been reborn. She could finally live her life with purpose and intention. At last, she knew where she was going, and her life would never be the same. As though swimming in an ocean of darkness, memories of two other ill-fated past lives engulfed her, and she felt herself drowning. If destiny had a voice, today it would be cruel laughter.

Remedy, Whalina, and Eva—three powerful women across three different lifetimes. Three lives dedicated to the same life purpose of stopping Tarquin and saving the kingdom. Two very much half-lived lives of unfulfilled dreams. Eva began to remember her life as Princess Remedy, the people she had loved, and the once eternal beauty of the kingdom.

The turmoil of Whalina's life, constantly feeling as though she was running out of time and destined for more, set to complete the damn painting. Whalina's naive dream to open her art gallery and, of course, her darling Neal, and what had become of their love? *Did he ever make it back to the kingdom, or did he make peace with what happened and moved on without me?* Eva's thoughts scrambled in her mind. She, of course, prayed for the latter, hoping her soulmate had managed to save himself and had found happiness on Earth, where the sun still shines.

Eva felt livid from bitter anger, an emotion she had never experienced. Filling Eva with blind, white-hot rage, blood rushed through her veins, arms, and legs, crawling with a thousand ants, itching to move, to do something. She held her hands over her recently broken heart as it was trying to shrink, to close its doors to any more unwanted memories, to protect itself from suffering. But deep down, Eva knew she couldn't close it, for closing her heart would mean closing to love, to joy, to light.

"It is both a blessing and a curse to feel everything so deeply." She recalled the quote from one of many treasured books and firmly resonated with the words today, as though the author had written them just for her and this moment in time.

Eva recovered her voice, stating boldly, as if Tarquin could hear, "This ends now." Her eyes burned like smouldering coals. She was determined to finish what she had started decades ago. Another life would not be sacrificed only for her to be placed back into this damned loop and forced to start again. She will bring the light back to the kingdom. She had been the saviour when her name was Remedy, and she was still that same girl. Until she fulfilled her life purpose, no other purpose would come, and her soul would never find peace and move on. Eva was certain this would be the life in which the kingdom would finally be liberated. It made sense. It had to. There was no other way.

The original painting she had begun as Remedy was finally completed to satisfaction, and Eva believed in no such thing as coincidence. She was ready, and the time was right. Whalina could not finish the painting, as she struggled with accepting darkness as part of herself. She believed herself to be good, fair, and just, and so bringing darkness into the soul of the painting, which she unconsciously knew was, in fact, her self-portrait, did not feel right.

Whalina could not bring herself to use a collection of colours. It had always been one singular colour: white, yellow, gold, or silver. Whalina could not risk mixing the paints or contaminating her soul. When Eva used red, the colour of temptation, she finally understood the lesson. People were neither good or bad; they were all on a spectrum of light. There was no such thing as darkness, only a lack of light, and so everyone was redeemable. Everyone who had strayed to the side of temptation with greed, hate, or anger in their heart could be saved with just a little more light. She had not yet understood the importance of that lesson and how it would help in conquering the kingdom, but she had faith that its meaning would be revealed in time.

In all her eighteen years of existing in the kingdom by the name Eva, she had not missed or yearned for anyone as much as she now did for her papa and mama. Their love was unmatched, and her heart ached when she considered what had become of Mama after Tarquin commandeered Papa's body—and, of course, the sweet babe she had carried.

The idea of her sister walking the land sparked a flame inside her soul, and with no time to waste, the orphaned girl decided she was and always had been Remedy. She was never alone, the kingdom had always been her inheritance, and her people had been waiting for far too long to be saved. *This is my home.*

Remedy took the slightly damp notepad containing the finished drawing and the scarce food reserves she had and set out on the three-day southern journey.

The passage was through forest and downhill mountain grounds, which were easy to walk on. Remedy met several frozen lakes and rivers, and for that, she was glad, for although swimming used to be Whalina's favourite pastime, in this lifetime, Eva had never swum. Thankfully, the closer she got to the coast, the warmer the temperature became, reminding Remedy of the last blazing summer she had experienced in the kingdom.

Tears again collected in her clear blue eyes as reminiscence of what could have been sparked a sensitive cord inside. Remedy remembered the very day when the sun did not rise, the fear of the people, and how she had led them to believe everything was and would remain just fine. She had left them unprepared, scared, and in the hands of a ruthless ruler. Remedy knew she looked different in this reincarnation, and they would not recognise her, yet she wondered how people would react if they discovered she was Remedy, the lost princess.

She didn't expect them to trust her—that would have to be earned—and she wouldn't be surprised if they wanted nothing to do with her. She expected for them to call her a liar and a coward, for they wouldn't believe the battles her soul had endured to be here today. Even for her, it all seemed almost too much to believe. The last time anyone had seen her was fifty years ago, at the amphitheatre when she had asked the public to hum with her and raise their vibrations of love. Perhaps those who had been present that day were now dead; maybe no one remembered and her whole existence had been forgotten.

Remedy tried to stay positive, fighting to keep her light alive, as she ventured closer to the darkness. By the morning of the third day, she had consumed all food supplies, yet even with an empty stomach and tired legs, Remedy continued. The sea was loud, raging in chaos, and she knew the coast was close.

Walking through the forest brought up feelings of déjà vu, as though she had walked this path before. She observed herself predicting the type or height of a tree a few feet in front and gasped when the eleventh guess in a row was correct. She figured this must have been an important place in her past life, yet searching her mind proved futile, as she could not find the path's significance. Remedy's memories felt like the most detailed and complicated mandala. Trying to separate pieces of the three lifetimes all woven together physically hurt her brain.

She tried to focus on the journey and continue ahead, until a stone path on the right made her hesitate. A strange sensation in her stomach caused her to stop and consider taking a turn to the darker pathway. It would mean changing course from the coast and venturing deeper into the forest. Remedy briefly considered the detour, but the sea was calling, compelling her to carry on.

Pushing the feeling aside, Remedy descended the mountain, finally becoming level with the sea. It was the first time in this lifetime when her young eyes saw the vast waters. A little overwhelmed by its boundless nature, Remedy was forced to stop, if only to watch its eternal greatness.

The moon shone brightly, reflecting the life of the sea. She did not know what she had been missing and had forgotten her love for water. Suddenly, memories of not only swimming in human form, but also the many years part of her soul had spent inside the whale flourished to surface. She had travelled millions of kilometres in the body of the biggest mammal in the world and with it, endless freedom.

With her heart already beating double time, Remedy sprinted. She let down her guard and forgot she was now in his territory as her legs were fuelled by excitement and love for the sea.

In the distance, a long pier took shape, and at the end of it stood a vague shadow.

Remedy stopped and tried to hold her breath, not to make a sound.

The figure did not seem to notice her as it looked across the ocean.

Watching her step, Remedy silently crept forward, observing the shadow take the shape of a tall man facing the sea, giving her the advantage of remaining concealed for a while longer. The worst of thoughts flooded her mind; with no plan of action or weapon, she was not armed to meet him. Other than the hearsay of the village, she knew nothing about her uncle or what he was capable of. Adrenaline rushed through her body, but she continued. Remedy knew she only had one shot at taking him down, and the element of surprise was important. He wouldn't dream of ever seeing her again, let alone see her go against him.

With faith that luck would stir in her direction, Remedy walked empty-handed towards a shadow that might or might not be him. Her feet were weak, and halfway down the pier, she was about to retreat, when the man turned around. Their eyes locked, and they stood motionless. As though the world had stopped, not even a flinch or blink of an eye could be detected.

His face was familiar, although different: aged and mature. The long grey beard had not been there before, and he had gained a noticeable mass about him. He smiled softly with his eyes, and Remedy responded with an uneasy smile of her own. In this lifetime, he was a stranger, but an inner voice of intuition told her that she could trust him.

Believing the man meant no harm, she stepped forward, and with it recalled the image of a bell or perhaps a flower. Another step forward, she could see his face clearly and a bell-shaped flower. The face finally found the right name. Wind. Remedy gained momentum as she raced towards him. Ready to meet his warm embrace, she eagerly opened her arms and unintentionally passed through him, falling from the edge of the pier into the cold seawater.

Remedy's eyes shot open in the darkness of the sea. It was like being thrown inside a black hole in space, a void with no air. Flailing and kicking, she finally brought her head above water. The once whale-spirited girl was drowning.

"Swim, Remedy, swim! Remember how to swim!" Wind shouted.

Remedy could remember the feeling of swimming, light as a feather, floating like a starfish at the surface. Feeling of safety, returning home, but that was all her old life; today, the very thing she used to love was killing her.

"*Hel-p me!*"

"I can't, Remedy! You … do this alone!" She heard the words between her scattered gasps for air.

No one was coming to the rescue; she was the saviour, and so she had to save herself. *What would Whalina do?* The girl who had spent hours in the water moved her feet and arms in a synchronised way, like a dance. Remedy tried kicking and moving her arms together. It took a couple tries, connecting the brain, breath, and body, then all at once, she was treading water.

With precise effort, she managed to swim towards the wooden pier and pull herself up. The abundance of air was welcomed into her starving lungs, and after a few moments, Remedy sat upright and saw that Wind was eager to speak.

"I am not here, Remedy, not in the physical sense that you are." As always, he was direct and to the point. "I live on Earth, and I have been coming here once a month as a projection, hoping for the off chance that you would find me." He stood awkwardly with his arms hanging by his sides, like a dead pendulum.

Remedy got onto her feet and slowly reached for Wind and his black cloak jacket. The shaman was right; her hand passed right through him.

"How did you know I would be here today?" Remedy twisted the excessive water from her hair and the beautiful wolf coat which would take weeks to dry.

"It's been eighteen years, and not a day passed when I didn't think of you, hoping you would wake up and finally remember. You are here, and it seems we are in great luck." His familiar smile reflected onto Remedy's face.

With every breath, Remedy had more questions but knew time was of the essence. What was most important was that Wind could help her figure out how to save the kingdom, as surely this was why he had come. Her heart was stronger than logic, and she couldn't help but ask, "What has become of my sister? Sarah." It was difficult to say the name; the last time her lips uttered the sound, Whalina had promised to create a new world for the dead and had not kept her word.

"She is alive, and so is Mikey and their two twin girls. Your parents have also not yet passed." Of course, the shaman knew what she had been thinking, and Remedy exhaled heavily in relief.

Death was on her side, and time was kind, for she still had a chance to prepare the afterworld for them. "Did Neal cross over?"

"It's been seventeen years since I last heard from him."

"You mean you did not send him to the kingdom? He did not follow me here?"

Remedy found herself confused. Previously, she had hoped Neal had saved himself and stayed back, refusing to acknowledge a small part of her that wished he was here. After all, he had promised to follow her to the kingdom, the same way Kai had come to Earth. He had said he would always find her, and she believed him.

"Remedy, there is something you need to know about Neal's soul. When a soul decides to voluntarily leave the Kingdom of Light and descend to a lower realm, one of pain and unconsciousness, it is almost always impossible to come back, and—"

"You said 'almost,' so there's a chance."

"No one ever has. You came back because half of your soul was inside the whale."

"Neal is forever enslaved to Earth. I will never see him again," she clarified to herself quickly. Flaming anger rose to her chest as she mourned another loss. Kai had ultimately sacrificed himself to spend their short time together on Earth. He had come to Earth to help her remember, to help her return; he was her lover, soulmate, and hero. Some losses you never get over, and this was one of them.

"Remedy, we tried, but after a year of ceremonies and rituals, he became weaker, and it had to stop." Wind was trying to lessen her grief, but the loss of a soulmate could not be cured; heartbreak was to be felt and lived through. "He did not want to stop trying, Remedy. He wanted to keep his promise, but it was killing him," Wind reassured her, but it was not his counsel that brought her back to the present moment. Wind's projection grew in transparency as time caught up with them.

"Everyone has a weakness. What is his?" Remedy refocused her attention.

"There is one thing he does not have."

"Light," she answered for them both.

The shaman nodded. "There is a reason why you had to leave the kingdom and return fifty years later. You preserved the original and untamed light from the kingdom." He paused, giving Remedy a moment to understand how special she truly was.

"When your soul went to Earth, it took the enlightened, divine light with it. When you combined with the other half that was living inside the whale, your soul became the brightest and most powerful soul in the whole realm." Wind allowed Remedy to take it all in.

The eighteen-year-old girl felt the gravity of her power and responsibility. Everything was up to her. The lives of millions were in her hands, and the future of all souls who had ever existed relied on her getting this right.

"That's not all. Tomorrow, at precisely eight twenty-three in the morning, a galactical gamma ray burst will occur. It will last only a few seconds and will shine a million trillion times as bright as the sun." He faded with every word that came from his mouth, yet he continued to explain. "Gamma ray bursts are the strongest and brightest explosions in the universe and are thought to be generated during the formation of black holes."

"Dark creates light," Remedy whispered to herself, whilst Wind continued to explain how the gamma ray bursts could produce as much energy as the sun in its ten-billion-year existence. "Wind, what do I need to do when the realm gets hit by the gamma ray?"

"You must unconditionally let your light shine, aiming to penetrate Tarquin's darkness. You want to beat him with love, Remedy. You have a weapon he never had." The shaman finally expired, and darkness once again surrounded Remedy.

CHAPTER 22

THE FACE OF LIGHT

Once Wind had vanished, an eerie feeling filled the space. The air was heavy with unspoken words and a thick fog approaching from the sea. Remedy was uncomfortable, standing on the pier alone, knowing *he* could be watching. She quickly gathered her wolf fur from the ground and headed back to land, but she realised there was nowhere to go.

The moon was halfway across the sky, so she still had around seven hours before the gamma rays enlightened the realm. She needed to stay close but far enough not to get caught. Naturally, her intuition guided her to the stone path, which she had descended some hours before.

Walking uphill, Remedy felt the wet fur slow her down. Out of breath, she paused to remove it, bringing the feeling of release as she shrugged the straining weight off her shoulders. Once upon a time, the fur had provided her with warmth and comfort. It was the one thing she had inherited from nature and called her own.

With a heavy weight on her heart, Remedy chose to leave the fur behind. It had served its purpose in the past, but now it had evolved into a burden, and to continue on her journey, she had to let it go. Somehow, she didn't feel the cold as she quickened her pace in complete silence.

Unavoidably, her mind drifted back to Neal and the possibility of him falling in love again. Aware that thoughts of this nature were nothing short of a distraction, she couldn't help but wonder whether he had become a father, naming his daughter after her like he had promised.

Remedy walked on the stone path in darkness for a while, giving her heart a taste of happiness as she imagined possible scenarios of her happily-ever-afters with Neal. A house in Cornwall, a dog and maybe even children of their own, afternoon tea, and countryside trips all felt out of reach, impossible to grasp or ever hold again. All of that and so much more had been lost. Remedy did not want to remember. It was easier to forget and leave her past lives behind. The last few days had been challenging without the addition of another lifetime worth of heartbreak.

At last, the stone path ended, bringing Remedy to the present, as an old wooden house became visible. A singular jasmine tree sat to the right of the house—the most beautiful tree Remedy had ever seen in the realm. One of its white flowers fell into her hand, and the calm wind brought a familiar sweet smell, and with it came feelings of nostalgia for something she could not yet remember. The wooden house was calling for attention.

She placed the flower behind her ear and entered, with the sound of wooden floorboards creaking under her feet. The abandoned place was one she had visited before. Only then it had been full of life. Remedy tried to remember whose house it was and what the young Princess Remedy would be found doing here, but no images or memories came. The rain, which had entered through a great hole in the roof, had badly damaged the green sofa, and the wallpaper had been ripped in several places. The curtains had been pulled down, and the windows were barricaded with wood. The old fireplace still had some burnt logs and ashes from the last time it had been lit. The dining table, set for two, was left untouched, with empty plates filled with dust and broken glass.

Remedy was uneasy, knowing the mournful sight had once been a well-looked-after loving home. *I shouldn't be here; this is wrong.* Step by step, she carefully walked backwards, until she tripped over a metal fork. On the broken wooden floorboards, she noticed a small photo of a girl laughing in a field of lavender plants. Remedy turned to the back and found a neatly written note: *2050 REMEDY, LAVENDER FIELD.*

She could see the resemblance between her former self and the woman she was today. Back then, her hair had been golden rich from the sun. Today, it was a few shades darker, more of a washed sandy colour. Yet the eyes were the same radiant ocean blue. Remedy put the picture inside her bralette, close to her heart.

Just as she was about to step outside, someone grabbed her hands and pressed her against the cold, musky wooden wall. "Who are you, and what are you doing here?" It was a male voice, with masculine solid hands around her wrists, which had been pulled to her lower back.

"Eva, my name is Eva. I'm just taking a walk," she replied quickly, figuring it was best not to declare her real name.

"Are you mocking me? Walks in the woods are not allowed. Now, again, what are you doing here?" He pressed her body harder to the wooden cabin wall, so close that Remedy could taste its earthy aroma on her tongue.

"I'm not from here. Please, you're hurting me!" Remedy tried to jerk herself away, whilst he remained silent and pressed her soft face into the wood.

He grabbed and pulled her hair, then pressed his thumb against the back of her neck, scanning her skin. "You don't have a number."

Remedy remembered Madeline telling her that those who lived in the South were marked with a number imprinted under the skin at the back of the head. This was so Tarquin's personnel could instantly identify people on the street to ensure everyone was accounted for and could be tracked.

Unsure of what to say, Remedy went with the honest route. "I'm not like anybody else. I'm not from here!" she shouted, partly from the force of being pushed against the rough wall and partly because she needed him to hear her out.

"I'm taking you in." He turned her back against the wall.

His face was not at all the masculine and hard features she had expected. The messy chestnut-coloured hair reached his shoulders and lightly blew over his forehead. Neither curly nor straight, it seemed they had the potential to be whatever they wanted to be. His lips were in a bowlike shape, with a straight bottom, while the top was curve shaped, pressed together with agitation. Yet what was most over-whelming for Remedy was his eyes. They reflected the moonlight, but their sparkle was gone, like looking inside an empty void. If she looked too long, she could get sucked into their sadness. His gaze was soft, and he looked surprised, somewhat lifted once he saw her face. The man did not look dangerous. He looked like he needed help.

"What happened to you?" she asked in a soft voice.

He hesitated, whilst Remedy noticed a small collection of water that had welled in his eyes. He appeared emotionally moved, as though no one had ever asked him that before. He replied by wrapping her arms across her chest, as though she was hugging herself, then bound her wrists towards each other with a coarse rope. This way she could not open her heart and use her light against him, leaving Remedy de-armed and vulnerable.

Those who still had some light left inside could, at any moment, spread their arms like eagle's wings and radiate love from their heart. The light could create an aura around oneself that was hard to penetrate and, if intended, could outshine an immense amount of darkness.

He yanked her forward, and they headed to the stone path and into the forest. The moon was behind them, meaning the gamma rays, her only hope, was about four hours away.

"Where are you taking me?" She protested by grounding her feet in place and not walking.

"To the palace prison. You seem the type who the king will want to meet personally," the man said with no enthusiasm. There was no personality or life inside of him, like he was acting on autopilot.

"And will he be there when I arrive?" Remedy asked, unsure of what answer she was hoping for.

"You weren't kidding. You are new here. Our king is our god; he will be the judge of your crimes and decide whether you will be sentenced to search for the king's stone or"—he stopped and took a breath—"your soul will be devoured. If it's worth consuming and if it's bright enough, he will extinguish your light and transmute it into darkness."

This was how he got stronger. Tarquin took every ounce of love and hope from people's hearts and transformed the energy into darkness.

For the rest of the journey, Remedy remained silent, planning ways she could free her arms and replaying what she would say to Tarquin. He was her uncle, after all, but in no way was he family. She wanted to understand why he had chosen the darkness. How could he take his only brother's life, and how, for fifty years, had he sought nothing but turmoil and destruction?

She had many questions but knew today was not about getting answers. Today was about putting an end to suffering and pain. It was time to rekindle both the metaphorical and physical light to the kingdom. Remedy was determined and believed she was strong enough to confront him. The love she held for the kingdom and its people, Neal, Sarah, and her family on Earth was more powerful than his anger and hate.

Yet, right now, her only hope was the man with no name. He had to free her arms. She had to win him over to the light; he had to help her. "May I please call you by your name?" she asked softly, hoping her kindness could give way to the light she hoped was still inside him.

"Phoenix," he murmured.

Before she had the chance to tame him some more, they arrived at the palace. Remedy remembered it being illuminated from the highest tower to the ground, but, of course, things had changed. There was no light. A smell of rotting flesh permeated the air as Phoenix escorted her towards the underground prison cells.

They stood behind the lake where she and Sacnicte had their last picnic, the place where the unicorns would drink at night, a sight which was now unheard of entirely. Darkness consumed the prison. She could not see where she was going nor what was around her. The putrid smell made her nauseated and reminded her of the time she had travelled through the forest in Hell. The stink of decaying bodies and the lingering smell of death made her wonder whether anyone was alive with her or if they had all died inside the prison.

Relying on her sense of hearing and the jiggle of keys, she figured they had arrived at her cell. Phoenix slowly pushed her inside the low-ceilinged cell, where she could not stand. Remedy fell on the cold, muddy earth, unable to get up, as her arms were still tied. The keys turned, and her heart raced at the speed of a thousand horses; she could not think clearly with a sense of impending doom hanging over her.

She rolled over on the grimy floor and shivered, feeling the retained memories of evil and the trauma of its previous occupants. Gradually, then all at once, Remedy was hyperventilating. She was used to the dark, but not like this—not with her arms tied around her body, unable to stand, in the house of a monster, with no moonlight to offer hope for a better tomorrow. She could not wait for the morning, for by then it would be too late. He would come, and she would be his prey, as he would take her life all over again. It seemed that her luck had run out.

"Phoenix, please don't leave me," she called out to the darkness and heard the words echo back. "Phoenix, please come back," she cried, trying to keep the tears from falling.

Remedy was afraid, terrified like never before. She finally understood how easy it was for Tarquin to destroy her people's faith. Even the strongest of hearts could break under his rule.

The sound of keys rang in her ears again, and a hand landed on her shoulder, helping her to sit upright. Phoenix lit a small candle. "I'm not supposed to be doing this."

Chapter 23

The Stars in the Sky

The candle burned throughout the night and into the early hours of the morning. When its light had finally expired, a cold shiver ran through Remedy's body, waking her into consciousness as fear knocked at the door of her heart. Her mind went to Neal. In that moment, she would do anything to be back in his arms, even if for a second, just to feel his warmth and breathe his smell. She felt the impending doom surrounding her. The air was moist with a thirst for her breath, and the icy earth beneath her was desperate for her flesh, for it, too, needed sustenance to survive. Remedy's heart was racing, eager to be set free.

All night she had been drifting in and out of sleep, hoping that by staying awake, she would not miss the gamma ray beams and the one chance at saving the kingdom. But that and so much more were out of her spectrum of control. The prison was pitch black, with no way of telling the time, and even if there was, Remedy's hands were still wrapped around her upper body.

"Phoenix," her voice trembled as she whispered to the darkness. "If you can hear me, please …" Remedy did not finish the sentence, because she did not know what words to use on the boy. He had to remove the rope, because if he didn't, she could already declare herself as good as dead. Tarquin will deplete her light and absorb her soul as he had done with countless before. The hopeless idea of telling him that she was his niece crossed her mind, but he had killed his brother with cold hands before; family meant nothing to the tyrant. Phoenix was her only hope. Somehow, he had to become her saviour first so she could be his after.

Remedy heard something like the rustling of dead leaves, followed by a gush of strong, bitter wind that seemed to go on forever. Finally, a crashing bang of the prison door stopped the draft of wind, and approaching footsteps bounced off the empty walls. They belonged to someone heavy and were neither steady nor smooth, thus they could not belong to Phoenix, for his long legs allowed him to stride effortlessly. A loud thump and an obnoxious chewing sound filled the prison cells' void. The ripping of old, hard flesh and the snorting tongue, which licked the trickling liquids from the side of the mouth, made Remedy's stomach turn. Although she could not see, the sounds were all too vivid to ignore. Besides, she was used to her mind creating images; living in the dark had made the imagination much more expansive.

The combination of smell and sound, the hungry earth eager to nibble on her skin, and the tiny cell were becoming too much to bear. If only she could breathe a little fresh air and feel the trunk of her oak tree, she could regain her strength and find the resilience to follow through with the path that destiny had put her on.

"Let me out." Remedy let the words rip from her throat, and at once, the vile consumption stopped.

Silence rested in the air, until the creature moved swiftly. It appeared next to the iron bars as the foul smell of spoiled meat came closer. With the clutter of rusty chains, a key that turned too fast, and without warning, Remedy was out of the cell, with the back of her hands pressed against the rough stone wall. The pain stung, but she pushed it aside, overridden with the sensation of something strangling her.

The creature's hairy arms were wrapped tightly around her neck, pressing with the weight of a thousand ocean rocks. The pressure was insufferable as he pulled her backward to the wall, dragging her naked feet off the dirty ground. The agony of trying to breathe exploded throughout her body, tormenting the mind as it knew there was no way out of the monster's grip.

An overwhelming buzzing rang in her ears so loudly that it forced everything else to be silenced. The darkness looked darker and felt warm—warm like home—and called her name. "Eva, *give in* …" The voice was old, and its depth was pulling her closer to the finish line of life. *"Don't fight it. Ease your pain, child."* The cunning voice won, and Remedy stopped fighting.

The warmth consumed her, taking her feet and legs, dissolving her bones into the grand, infinite space of the universe. Just as it was getting ready to enter and rupture the heart, her feet touched the ground, and Remedy gasped air into her crumbling lungs. Her body welcomed the previously thought-to-be stale air, recolouring her pale skin. Too weak to get up, Remedy lay on the muddy ground, listening to the heavy footsteps by her side.

"I decide who lives and dies," a familiar voice said. It was raspy, confident, and chilling, sending goosebumps down Remedy's newly received body. The creature yelped in pain, and even though he had been moments from suffocating her to death seconds before, Remedy found an ounce of empathy for his suffering.

Being unable to cover her ears, for her own sake, Remedy prayed for the high-pitched scream to end. It seemed to go on for hours; when in reality, it was moments. Time was always an illusion. It stopped, and a warm liquid trickled over the ground, lukewarm and smelling of rust and metal.

"It reeks. Clean it up. I like 'em pure inside and out."

Remedy finally remembered the voice. She had met Tarquin twice before, once in the woods and in her house, whilst he was occupying Papa's body. Paradoxically, he had just saved her life, even if he intended to take it himself in the next few hours. Remedy lost track of his steps, then the prison doors closed with a loud bang, startling her. From nowhere came arms that gently helped her up to her shaking feet.

"Maybe it would have better if the creature had taken your life," Phoenix said in a low, sad tone.

"Phoenix, what is the time?"

"You are about to die a painful death and have your life essence sucked out of you. What do you care for the time?" He guided her from the dungeon to outside, under the starless sky.

Remedy looked for the moon, but wherever it was, it was not here. "Please, I must know."

"It's nearly eight in the morning. You should already be at the amphitheatre." His voice had changed tone.

If Remedy had more experience of talking to people who cared about her in this lifetime, she might be confident enough to say the boy cared for her fate.

"Don't try anything." Phoenix untied her wrists. "Your light doesn't work within the palace perimeters."

After several hours of having her arms wrapped around her body, Remedy finally spread them like wings. She felt free as a bird with the rush of adrenaline that ran down her body. She was in the position to strike Phoenix, who had momentarily turned his back. Or she could just run to the woods, to the north, and forget about her purpose and kingdom. She wasn't exactly unhappy living with the loyal oak tree. No one was forcing her to fight and risk her life. There was beauty in the life she had been living, and it was easier to leave things as they were rather than fight and chance losing it all. But the stakes were too high. She would never turn back without knowing she had tried and given all she could.

Phoenix turned to face her. "Take your clothes off."

The moment had passed, and she had stayed. Behind him was an old ceramic bath, filled to the top with crystal-clear water.

"It belonged to the princess before she fled the kingdom and left her family and people behind," Phoenix murmured.

"Princess Remedy? You knew her?" Remedy asked with fury. Her name and legacy had been tarnished; people must think of her as nothing more than a coward and traitor.

"It was before I was born, but I heard stories. Now get into the bath. We don't have time," Phoenix said, leaving Remedy with more questions than they would ever have the time for. Phoenix looked to the side as she stripped naked and entered the lukewarm water, which quickly turned murky from the mud and blood she had been wearing.

"Do you believe Remedy abandoned the kingdom?"

"I don't blame her if she did."

"But do you think she willingly left everyone at his mercy?" She stepped out of the bath and dried her body with the rough cloth left on the side.

Phoenix turned around, perhaps to ensure his prisoner was not making a run to the woods or to simply glance at her bare body. For the first time, their eyes interlocked as they looked into the windows of each other's souls. Standing only a few centimetres apart, without being restrained, Remedy felt her blood pumping faster and was sure Phoenix could feel it too. He could probably see it too, as she felt herself blush.

He no longer looked at her with distrust or pity. Kindness and care hid behind his forest-green eyes. "Maybe she didn't have a choice … I don't know." He handed her a wool robe, breaking their gaze. He again looked to the side, allowing her privacy as she clothed her body.

"I have to tie your arms, Eva." The words reluctantly rolled off his tongue as he stepped closer.

"If you do that, you are sentencing me to death," she said with a glare. Remedy hoped the humanity she saw in Phoenix was real. She prayed that light resided inside him.

"He will kill you either way." He grabbed her arms, resisting Remedy's futile struggle, for he was much stronger than her and seemed to know the way around human combat and capture.

Remedy dragged her feet towards the amphitheatre to buy herself more time with Phoenix. She could see his walls were breaking and that he had it in him to set her free. Despite Tarquin's conditioning on the peoples' psyche, deep down, they still held a light. Regardless how small, it was hope. Remedy saw it in Phoenix, and surely, he was not the only exception.

As they left the palace quarters where no light could live, her heart thundered, and she felt the light inside get bigger and warmer, eager to radiate out. It was a strange feeling, one she had never experienced before. Remedy espied Phoenix, and it became stronger, as though an explosion of light was happening inside her chest. Of course, she had felt her light before and would allow it to shine when she saw Madeline, but this was different. The light's magnitude was stronger, more abundant, and eager to connect with his light. Its power was overwhelming, creating butterflies inside her stomach and making her feet unsteady.

"Time, please?" she asked, trying to stay focused.

"You're obsessed." He checked his wooden watch. "It's ten past eight."

Remedy's heart skipped a beat. She had seen this watch before—not on Phoenix's hand but in a previous lifetime. "Where did you get your watch?"

"I found it at the place where I found you," he quickly answered, as though something agitated him inside. "That wooden cabin. I don't know why, but I go there sometimes. Now, stop talking; we're here." His voice turned cold as he put on his brave face.

In the eyes of the people, he was nothing more than Tarquin's slave. He was doing the most hated job in the kingdom, capturing innocent souls so Tarquin could kill their light and get stronger himself.

People of all ages and walks of life filled the amphitheatre, but they all had something similar. They were all tired and worn out— skinny, with pale see-through skin and red eyes. Remedy searched for someone she might know from her previous life but quickly realised that even if those people were still alive, they would look different now and be hardly recognisable. The place that had once been filled with joy and laughter was utterly silent as the fear-filled people were forced to watch the execution of one of their own.

Walking behind Phoenix to the centre of the stage, Remedy tried to make eye contact with as many people as possible, striving to connect with them, ease their pain, and give them hope. She desperately wanted to tell them who she was and that they had not been abandoned.

Some regarded her with pity. Others could not meet her eyes at all.

"I hereby bring you, Eva, a wanderer from the north who thought she could break the rules and live in the kingdom without serving our king," Phoenix said boldly.

Remedy glanced at his watch. Seven minutes until the gamma beam rays hit the atmosphere, and her arms were still tied back. "Phoenix, please trust me. You must untie me now," she whispered ever so quietly, as not to diminish his status in front of the crowd.

He turned towards her with a soft gaze, and she knew that although he wanted to, he could not free her.

The ocean that stood behind them roared wildly, and the sound of crashing waves made it seem as though they were much closer to the coast than they were. Nature responded in all the ways it could as Tarquin lurked from the shadows, surrounded by heavy black fog, and sauntered onto the stage.

A gust of wind blew towards Remedy, attempting to shake her balance, but she stood firmly. She had waited for this moment for decades, imagining the face of the monster who had run her homeland to the ground. But when Tarquin took the black satin cloak off his head, he looked nothing like the demon Remedy had envisioned.

He had a certain masculinity about him, contributed by his well-defined jawline and the most symmetrical face that ever existed. His unfathomable golden-brown eyes contrasted exceptionally with his light-toned face, and above were perfectly moulded eyebrows, like two fat caterpillars precisely the same length. His coal-black hair blew back with the wind, leaving traces of black dust. It seemed he was breathing with his whole body, and with every exhale, he released more dark dust into the tension-filled air. Within seconds, a black carpet of ashes coated the ground around him. Remedy could not believe someone so beautiful could be so rotten inside. Tarquin fixated on the crowd, who did not dare look into the devil's eyes.

His thick lips tried to curve into a smile, but the muscles did not know how. Finally, he managed to smile with his mouth, leaving his eyes cold, and called out to the gathered people. "Look at me!"

His subjects raised their heads, and his lips again attempted to curve into a smile.

Remedy tried to stay calm, remembering that fear feeds the darkness. She told herself she needed to stay brave, now more than ever, then she heard the voice in her head. *Courage, this is your destiny. Believe in yourself.* The smell of blooming flowers filled her senses as she felt her ancestors beside her.

She flitted her eyes to Tarquin and glared into his cold eyes. Inside, she saw the terrified faces of the thousands of souls he had captured.

He blinked once, and they were gone. "I know you," he said, inching towards her, penetrating her ocean-blue eyes, and the obsidian rug of dust followed closely behind him. "You're not like the rest of them." He stopped walking and narrowed his gaze at her, as though he could not believe his eyes. "Liiiigh–t. You can generate it. Who are you?" The words fell from his mouth like a snake's tongue.

Remedy felt her breath catch in her throat. "I'm nobody," she finally answered, tactfully moving her fingers, hoping the one person who needed to see them was paying attention.

"Don't lie to me! Why is she still standing, you pathetic animal? Onto her knees!" Tarquin roared at Phoenix. A loud thunder bang followed his words, shaking the ground.

Phoenix hit Remedy's knees with a stick, bringing her to kneel before the King of Darkness, and he swiftly pulled the rope and loosed the grip on her hands.

Remedy subtly freed her arms but kept them back; all that she needed now was the gamma rays.

"Where did you find her?"

"In an abandoned wooden cabin, north of the city," he answered, though his voice was shaky.

Remedy looked at the large town clock behind the crowd. Two minutes remained before the sky would be illuminated. Wind had said the explosion of gamma rays would only last a few seconds, and Remedy had to time her light expansion with the universe. Locking her eyes with Tarquin and without opening her arms, Remedy slowly got to her feet.

Tarquin stood speechless and motionless. The king held his breath, suspending the dark dust in the heavy air. His face turned pale, and lips parted slightly, numb with words, as he saw someone defy his orders for the first time in fifty years.

Ignoring him, Remedy stood firmly planted on the ground with Phoenix close by, for she liked to think she could trust him. With a minute to go, Remedy had to do one more thing before she opened her heart to the darkness. "My name is Remedy, the lost Princess of the Kingdom of Light," she said boldly, igniting a loud awe amongst the crowd. "I have been murdered by Tarquin and have reincarnated to fulfil my purpose and be the saviour I was always destined to be. I am a guardian of the light."

Tarquin no longer wore the same stamp of external beauty as he did before. He had turned sickly pale. Remedy knew he was afraid. She had a chance.

"I am here to take back what you stole."

He scanned her body from head to toe, then let out a loud mocking laugh, making Remedy's muscles clench as she recalled the memory of his cruel laughter when he had seized her papa's body.

"Is this how you say hello to your uncle?" He continued his cunning laughter, taking no notice of the tiny specks of the blazing gamma rays approaching from behind.

"This is how I say goodbye." Remedy spread her arms as wide as an eagle's wings, opening the portal of her heart, releasing generations of stored light.

A fountain of white matter exploded from the centre of her chest, holding the purest light containing nothing but love. Remedy's love was nothing short of selfless, as she had willingly sacrificed her life for the divinity that lived inside the whale, then readily left her life on Earth for the good of the kingdom and its people. Remedy's love was pure and good at its core. She was the most generous and benevolent being in the whole realm, and nothing could match her desire of returning light and love to the kingdom.

The white light threw Tarquin to the ground and pulled the long black cape off his back. The King of Darkness blocked the light by opening his arms, which spread into large raven wings. The black-feathered wings consumed most of the space on the stage, making it look far too easy for him to consume Remedy's soul. He approached her without a scratch, whilst it seemed that despite Remedy giving it her all, it would not be enough to beat the impenetrable demon.

"You failed before, and you will fail again," Tarquin sang in a mocking tone.

Blood dripped from her nose, and the light she was expelling was mixing with his darkness.

"Just like your parents, you are weak. You are pathetic. I will take your life, as I had taken theirs!" He marched towards Remedy with a colossal dark smog.

The words sparked a flame of anger and spite for the horrific deeds he had committed. The emotions of hate ran through her veins, and the darkness infected her heart. Tarquin was winning. Like a parasite, he had gotten under her pure skin and filled her with guilt and shame, for she had failed not only her family but the entire kingdom and universe. He had gotten inside her mind, flashing images of all the people who had died at his hands because of her failure to be the saviour. Her beloved Mama did not even get a burial. He had thrown her into the ocean with the unborn babe.

"You are too late, Remedy. You let them all down, and you're about to do it again." Tarquin laughed, pulling at all her sensitive cords.

In the corner of her eye, she saw Phoenix's hands extend forward to take the darkness inside of him to lessen the amount that would strike her. The boy whom she had known for less than a day was ready to lose his life for her. Remedy understood that Phoenix was not just Phoenix. He was Neal and Kai reincarnated. Whether or not he knew who he was, he had found a way back to her.

Remedy's heart exploded with love for her people, who stood both terrified and excited with hope for the possibility of living in light again. Her love doubled, and then tripled, as she thought of Mama and Papa, and, of course, Sarah, Teresa, and Edward. She could feel Sacnicte's presence, as though she was standing beside her.

Remedy's light pierced the monster's skin, infecting him with his most-feared human attribute: love.

Love is the driving force of making the impossible possible. To love means to let go of fear and surrender into the unknown where all doors are open. For that to happen, one must truly accept themself. They must find peace within and let go of the past, forgive themselves for their mistakes and for not knowing better at the time. They must let go of insecurities and imperfections so when they love, they love with freedom and no boundaries, for love is infinite, undefined, and unstoppable.

Love poured like the world's greatest waterfall from Remedy's heart, and when the gamma beam rays illuminated the sky for only a few seconds, all went white, and time stopped. White light burst into every corner of the universe, no stone went unturned, and all beings bathed in its glory. The hearts of the nation's people opened, and, at last, every man, woman, and child could finally feel that which they had been forced to shut off: love.

Smiles and tears of joy and gratitude spread like wildfire amongst the crowd and travelled into the kingdom's far north, east, and west. The emotions were raw, but no one was afraid, as they trusted in the returned saviour. They were lost but now have been found. Love which, as always, lived inside could, at last, come forward to the surface.

The gamma rays dispersed into the air, but Remedy's body stayed illuminated, shining from the inside whilst connected by a golden cord with Tarquin. She injected him with love, forgiving him for killing her parents and baby sister, forgiving him for destroying what her ancestors had protected and nurtured for aeons—forgiving him, for he had lost his way.

Remedy's love was more powerful than his hate, and it was love that allowed his soul to peacefully leave his body. The black wings turned into dust, and his body shrunk, until the last piece of ash dissolved in her light.

Curled in a ball, Remedy lay on the ground, breathing ever so softly. She could hear the joy in the cries of her people as the decades of suppressed emotions flowed freely and, at last, knew her purpose had been completed. Her eyes opened, and her gaze landed on Phoenix, who too had a glow around his face and eyes that shined so brightly.

"Princess Remedy, forgive my ignorance. I had no idea—"

Remedy pulled him towards her and kissed him deeply. She could feel his soul inside her, and everything else disappeared. It felt like they were both on the cusp of eternity and the dawn of existence, and all their memories and hopes for the future collided. She ran her fingers through his silky hair, the same as when he had been her Neal and when she had lived the life of Whalina. Remedy wanted the moment to last forever, so she pulled him closer so their physical hearts could sync and beat together just one more time.

His lips tasted like strawberries and warm summer evenings; he was a dream come true, and all she needed to find her final resting peace.

"Remedy, what's wrong, my love?"

Salty tears streaked her face, and Remedy knew he remembered.

"You found me. How did you find me?" Remedy tried to speak clearly because she did not know how much time remained for them.

"I made a deal to serve him for as long as I shall live, and he brought me back. He wiped my memories." He looked down with a speck of sadness and regret in his bright eyes.

"No, don't feel guilty. You did what you had to. Thank you." She cupped his face into her hand. Remedy bit her lips, wishing she could say something more. "Phoenix. I must go." She stifled her tears and drowned out the rest of the world. It was just her and him.

"Go? Go where? I just got you back." Phoenix pulled her closer.

"I'm dying. My heart is slowing down. My purpose is complete." Her words were breaking, and although Phoenix tried to interrupt, Remedy placed her finger over his lips so she could continue.

"Where I'm going, you cannot follow, but I will be watching over you every single night. You just need to look up to the sky, and you will see me. I will be waiting for you, and once you fulfil your purpose, together we will rule the sky."

Remedy smiled and felt his previously tight arms around her loosen its grip. She faded as her ashes floated skywards. Her physical body turned into cosmic matter, and her love turned into light. A blanket of stars stretched to infinity as Remedy paved a path for souls to cross over into their new reincarnation. She would be their guardian and would give a piece of her light to each soul to take with them back on Earth.

The dark night sky would never be starless again.

Epilogue

The birds sang their favourite birdsong, and all animals raced to the tallest of mountains to see, at last, what they had missed the most. The sun slowly rose from the horizon, and hundreds of kilometres of forests turned to face its light.

At first, people had to cover their eyes, because they were not accustomed to the beauty of the light. For some, it would be their first time being in the presence of something bigger than a candleflame. Slowly, they would peek between their fingers and marvel at the sun's solar power, and when the sun took its rest, they found peace knowing the Guardian of Light would forever watch over them in the night.

About the Author

Maja Mika has Polish origins and grew up in North London. After studying film at the University of Surrey, and briefly working in TV, she was convinced there was more to life and embarked on a solo trip to Rishikesh, India, the birthplace of yoga.

Today she is a yoga teacher, breathwork facilitator, and spiritual retreat holder. After traveling to Ecuador, where she studied with Shamans and acquired knowledge in plant medicine, she could no longer keep the story of Whalina to herself, feeling compelled to write *Beneath The Surface Of Light*.

Inspired to share spiritual concepts and wisdom with readers who otherwise may never ponder the bigger picture, Maja believes she can reach a wider audience through fiction. She has always enjoyed writing and, from a young age, created short stories and poetry.

In her spare time, she enjoys reading, walking her dog Coco, swimming in the sea, watching black-and-white films, and exploring new places in nature. And, of course, writing her next work of fiction.

Printed in Great Britain
by Amazon

22681976R00128